Tilly's Story

Diane Guntrip

To Dennis,
For his unwavering support and encouragement.

Thank you to the following people:
to Brenda and Jenette
for their superb proof-reading skills,
to April for her expert advice on social media and her
invaluable knowledge on all things teen-related,
to Steve Barwick from All In One Book Design
for his expertise in book design,
to Dr Philip Murray for his inspiring rendition of
Morceau de Concours by Gabriel Fauré.

Chapter 1

Tilly turned her head to look at the clock again, three in the morning and she was still wide awake. Only three more hours before the alarm would shriek into action. So far she hadn't slept a wink. Panic flooded through her body as her mind raced over all the items on the list of things she had to complete by the end of that day.

Life at St Celia's Academy of Music for Talented and Gifted Students was full-on. Tilly was a boarder there and a talented music student majoring in flute. It was her final year. She had set her sights high and planned to continue her flute studies, after graduating from the Academy, at an overseas Conservatoire. At the top of the list were the Conservatoire de Paris and the Royal School of Music in London.

The morning at St Celia's, which the students had shortened to St C's, was taken up as usual with academic lessons. It was an early morning start at 8 o'clock, finishing in the afternoon at 2 o'clock sharp. This was to allow time for the students to attend their specialist music lessons in the ultra-modern specially designed Music Block. This was referred to as the Block and was the pride and joy of both staff and students alike. It was there that the students would meet with their private tutors for specialized music lessons, followed by intensive practice in the individual soundproofed rooms. If a concert was looming, which appeared to be often, then there would be orchestral rehearsals to fit in as well.

To make matters worse, there was the proposed advanced Italian class to be squeezed into Tilly's hectic schedule. This would be taken by Signora De Luca, known by the students as, *the vision in purple* or more commonly as *the vision*. Small in height but rather broad elsewhere, she always wore layers and layers of different shades of purple chiffon which floated around her. This outfit was matched by jangly bracelets in shades of violet through to aubergine which were studded with glittering gems. Reaching half-way up her plump arms, the clinking jewellery announced her arrival.

She seemed to think Tilly had a special gift with the Italian language and had been trying to convince her to take an extra class. 'There you are!' she had screeched. 'I've been looking for you everywhere. I really need you to make a decision as soon as possible. Time is running out. Two extra sessions a week would make all the difference.'

Tilly had responded as she always did, by smiling politely and saying, 'I'll think about it.' She would have turned around and walked away in the opposite direction even if it wasn't the way she had planned to go. She always looked so in control even though inside she was quivering with fear.

Her workload was already pushing the limits and Tilly felt, that if anyone else placed extra demands on her, she would scream and not be able to stop. She was already at breaking point.

Tilly's mind raced back to her unending list for the day. Following her normal weekly Italian class, there was her flute lesson with Mr Ford. Now retired from his busy life as a professional flute player, Jack Ford was the ideal teacher for Tilly. Short in stature, with an unkempt beard, and a cheeky grin, he delighted in bringing a smile to Tilly's face. He always insisted on referring to her by her full name, Matilda. Normally, she would have frowned at that but, because it was Jack, she excused him. He recognised that she was exceptionally gifted and he looked forward to the day when she would also stand tall on the world stage.

Jack Ford was a teller of stories. At the completion of her lesson, he liked nothing better than to fill her mind with tales of his professional life, when he had been a visiting professor at one of the state's top universities. She also learnt that in between his lecturing appointments, he had spent time accompanying top vocal artists on stage as well as performing in his own right. He was classed as being a world-famous flautist so she counted herself lucky to have Mr Ford as her tutor. It was even rumoured, he had accompanied, on more than one occasion, a famous Italian male vocalist when he had recorded his CDs. Tilly was never sure whether his stories were true. Normally, she loved her lessons with Jack and counted down the hours to when her lesson was due but not today.

Today, the list in Tilly's head seemed to go on forever. So did the uncontrollable flowing river of fear and dread that was engulfing her whole being as she lay in bed. She just couldn't go on like this for much longer. She knew she couldn't. Night after night she had spent wide awake tossing and turning from one side of the bed to the other.

To Tilly, it seemed as though her mind had taken on a personality of its own over which she had no control. She had always had a vivid imagination. Now it was working overtime. Terrifying thoughts raced around so fast she was unable to keep up with them. When they reached their peak, at around three o'clock in the morning, it was then that the height of the panic really set in. Her thoughts took over to produce the most horrifying images. Pictures which resulted in the frightening panic attacks where she found herself sitting bolt upright in bed, her breathing totally out of control. One moment she was shivering and the next she was clammy with perspiration.

These attacks were the scariest of all. She was frightened that one night, she wouldn't recover from one of these attacks that left her gasping for air. With her imagination running wild, she had visions of being found, alone in her room in the morning. When it was noticed she'd failed to arrive in the dining room downstairs for breakfast, she imagined Amy, her best friend, banging furiously on her door and shouting, 'Tilly, open the door! Tilly!'

She could just imagine everyone on the corridor racing to see what was happening. She saw the expressions of horror written across their faces. Jessica especially, who was well known for overreacting, would be sure to cause more mayhem by dramatically fainting as Tilly's limp body was carried out on a stretcher.

When morning eventually arrived, with its bright sunlight filtering through the thin yellow curtains, Tilly was to be found, as usual, kneeling on the cold tiles in her ensuite bathroom. Her head was stuck over the toilet bowl, where she was being violently sick. 'No! Not again! Please not again!' she gasped as she grabbed her face flannel and made an attempt to wipe her damp, clammy face.

The continual worry, nausea accompanied by vomiting and the lack of sleep, had begun to take its toll. When Tilly looked at herself in the mirror it was obvious to her how dreadful she looked. She had always been petite with delicate features. She wasn't a beauty. However, her huge hazel eyes, long lashes, and her finely arched eyebrows were the features that had made her stand out in a crowd.

There wasn't much to smile about at the moment. If her recent weight loss was so obvious to her, what must other people be thinking? This was not helped by the dark circles under her hazel eyes and her almost colourless lips.

Recently, Tilly had spent a lot of time staring at herself in the mirror in her tiny ensuite. To an observer, one would have thought she was obsessed with her appearance, perhaps not unlike a lot of teen girls who spend ages taking selfies and posting them on Instagram for the entire world to see. On closer inspection, one would have realised that there was no camera or phone in sight, no images plastered on her Instagram page. No, Tilly's thoughts were miles away.

Tilly was in another world far away, a recurring nightmare. Her own pale, thin features were replaced by a vision of her mum and how she had appeared weeks before she had succumbed to the ravaging illness that had claimed her life. Losing her mum had broken Tilly's heart into fragments so minute she felt they could never be mended.

Apart from Tilly's physical sickness, there was a cavernous hole inside her. It was as though all the joy of youth, the hopes and aspirations, and the excitement of living had been sucked out of her leaving her empty. 'Blot it out,' she said as she tightly shut her eyes and clenched her fists. 'Blot it out. Go away!' However, this image wasn't the only thing on Tilly's mind that she wanted to 'Blot out'.

Tilly had often thought how great it would be if there was a switch you could flick on which would have returned her to the life she so vividly remembered. The life before her mum had become so ill. 'Oh, Mum, I miss you like crazy. I don't know what you'd think of me now! I need you so much. I don't know what Dad will do when he finds out. I'm SO scared. I need you now.'

Unfortunately, for Tilly, no switch existed. A terrifying jolt brought her back to the present. Reality set in as another wave of nausea surged through her body and she flung herself down on the floor in front of the toilet bowl for the third time that morning.

Chapter 2

The Previous Year

Jo, Tilly's mother, knew her time was limited. Her journey was coming to its end – far too early. She had been given plenty of warning of its arrival. However long she had left would not be enough. Nevertheless, she kept these thoughts to herself. It was too painful for her to put them into words and share them with her family.

This particular sunny afternoon was unusually warm for the time of year. Through her bedroom window, she could gaze out at the pure blue Australian sky, the floating fluffy clouds and she revelled in the sight. It was now late autumn and the garden was recovering from the heat of summer and relishing in the pre-winter showers. She delighted in watching out for the native bandicoots as they raced around the garden often stopping to furiously dig when they had found fungus, worms or grubs to devour. They mostly appeared in the cool of the day and if you sat very still, they would come quite close. Once, she had been able to sit on the ground watching whilst they nibbled at the birdseed she had scattered at her feet. Now she only had the strength to sit and absorb the nature around her, the huge towering eucalypts and the visiting native birds.

Today, she was propped up by pillows in the reclining armchair in the bedroom she shared with her husband Pete. It was a very important afternoon for Jo. She was awaiting the arrival of her best friend, Stephie, whom she had known since her uni days. These two women went back a long way. They had great memories of their times when they had studied to become teachers. There had been an instant rapport. Both had shared the same interests and more importantly, the same sense of humour. Now, they knew each other inside out and could say whatever they wanted to each other without causing offence.

In appearance, they were the complete opposites. Jo was always the petite one with the delicate features and sparkling hazel eyes, features she had passed on to her daughter Tilly. Stephie, on the other hand, always gave the appearance of being so physically strong with bright blue eyes, a crop of unruly blonde hair and a ready smile.

Both graduates had gone on to become teachers. Jo had met Pete and they had married. However, Stephie had never met the man of her dreams and although she had had numerous boyfriends, had remained single. Jo had encouraged her best friend to buy a house just down the road from where she and Pete had settled with their two young children, Tilly and Dan. Not long after Stephie had secured a teaching post at the same school as Jo. She was more than a friend, more of an honorary member of their compact family. She had babysat the children when they were tiny and they always referred to her as Auntie in their pre-teen days.

Whenever Stephie was around, there was always lots of fun and laughter. This was what Jo desperately needed. She had found out the hard way that whenever friends and relatives had learnt that she had cancer, their attitude towards her had changed. At first, they were all very sympathetic and had offered to help, but as time had gone on, their visits had become less. Now that her time was limited to weeks, they didn't know what to say. They found difficulty in looking her in the eye and so they stopped visiting and making those important phone calls.

Stephie wasn't like that. She talked about everyday matters and funny things that had happened to people that they both knew. She reminded Jo of the good times and they would sit and laugh until tears ran down their faces.

Today was important. Jo realised her family was finding it hard to come to terms with her illness and especially, acknowledging that she wouldn't always be around.

Since her cancer diagnosis five years earlier, she had passed through so many hurdles her illness had thrown in her direction. Each time there had been a certain amount of success followed by a setback. She had approached the next hurdle with courage and strength determined that she would win. Her aim was to reach the goal post of being cancer-free and win with flying colours. There was no other option for Jo. She had everything to live for, a devoted husband and family.

Until recently she had flatly refused to even consider the possibility that one day she wouldn't be there for them. It had not been easy, far from it. She would not admit to her family, not even to Pete, how hard she had had to fight and was still fighting. With Stephie, she could let down her guard and tell her friend how it really was. She didn't mind Stephie seeing her with tears streaming down her face as she grasped onto her best friend's hand like a vice.

However, her most recent talk with her oncologist had confirmed that she needed to, 'Get her affairs in order'. This was what she planned to do that afternoon.

Her tall, strong husband wasn't coping well. When she thought about it, were any of them? She knew Pete was still devoted to her, but she had noticed a definite shift in his behaviour. Yes, he was still attentive. Yes, he would do anything she asked. However, she sensed a withdrawal. He seemed to be keeping something back from her. It was something she could sense. She didn't need to ask him but she knew he was mentally preparing himself for when she wasn't there.

This afternoon, Jo needed Stephie's support more than ever. She needed her to help plan her funeral. Whenever she mentioned it to Pete, he'd kept shying away from the task. 'But it's got to be done,' she had implored him but he didn't want to acknowledge it.

'Talk to Stephie,' he had at last suggested, so that was what she was going to do.

When Stephie arrived that afternoon she was carrying a huge bunch of flowers – a gift from the staff at school. It broke her heart to see her best friend huddled in the armchair, propped up by numerous cushions looking as though she'd flop over like a rag doll without them. Stephie hoped Jo wouldn't notice the initial expression of shock on her face. Her best friend had lost even more weight and was so pale and lined. She appeared like a woman of at least twenty years older than her forty-seven years. Was it only a few days since she'd called in?

Stephie thought back to the time when she'd played a part in the local drama group. 'Help,' she thought to herself. She tried to remember how she had then got into character because she was being forced into acting out her biggest part this afternoon. She produced the brightest smile she could muster, placed the flowers in a safe spot and went over to her friend and gave Jo the biggest hug. It was then she thought she couldn't go ahead. Her friend was so thin, almost birdlike. She buried her head in Jo's arms, blinked back the tears and forced herself to smile. 'Even if your face aches,' she told herself, 'keep smiling.' How desperately she wished she could have been anywhere else that afternoon!

Jo may have been physically weak but she had a will of iron. She instructed Stephie to pick up the paper and pen left in readiness on the bedside table and to come to sit next to her. She began without hesitation. 'I want everyone to remember the good times, the fun times. I want bright, joyful music. I want songs that people know and can sing along to, none of those hymns that drag on and on. I've made lists so don't worry. I want everyone in dresses in bright colours, definitely not black.'

Stephie quipped in with her own sense of humour. 'Even the men?'

It brought a smile to Jo's face and lessened the tension.

'I can't see Pete in a dress can you?' she replied. 'Well, not in bright colours!' replied Stephie jokingly.

'I plan to look down on you all and watch so make sure you get it right,' she declared.

Stephie looked at her best friend, her eyes wet with tears.

'Oh, don't you start crying. It's got to be done. Pete doesn't want to discuss it and I'll ask the children for their input later when we've got the basics.'

Stephie gulped, swallowed hard and asked, 'Well, can you give me a list of the music you'd like?'

'It's over there on the cabinet.'

Stephie need not have worried. Her friend was organised as ever, even if the scribbled names of the songs showed how shaking her hands had become.

'How many songs are you planning to have?' she asked in astonishment as Jo began reading out the list. 'It sounds more like a party.'

'That's just what I want except, I wish I could be there.' Looking up she saw that Stephie was going to lose it again and said with resignation, 'Well, I've had lots of spare time to think about it.'

With bewilderment, Stephie sighed, 'But what about Pete and the children? Surely they've got ideas of what they want to happen?'

Jo ran her hands through her thinning hair, which was no longer dark and shiny with the chestnut streaks she was known for. She showed signs of exasperation twisting her gold wedding band around her thin finger and stated, 'Pete says I'm to do whatever I want. I'm finding it so hard with him at the moment. He doesn't want to acknowledge it's going to happen. Help him?'

'You know I'll always be there for them, for Pete and the children.'

'I'm so worried about leaving the children; St C's has been so good. They are allowing Tilly home to spend time with me just before ... '

It was then that Jo was completely lost for words

and then both women were engulfed in heartfelt tears.

Later, after a cup of tea, Jo, now tired, managed to whisper, 'One thing that brings me peace is knowing that you'll always be there for Dan and Tilly. For that, I'm forever grateful. They will always have you to turn to.'

With that, the tears flowed again.

Chapter 3

Gillie Longhirst was one of the Housemothers in charge of the female boarders at Grantham House where Tilly had a room on the second floor. St C's took in students from around the world so needed boarding facilities for those students who lived far away. All the girls under her care adored Gillie. She was likened to the favourite aunty that everyone wished they could have. When she wasn't teaching Song Writing, where she was to be referred to as Ms Longhirst, the girls of Grantham House were allowed to call her Gillie. The popular Housemother was friendly with a lovely open smile and such deep brown eyes. She wore her fair hair in a ponytail and dressed in jeans, sweatshirts, and sneakers when she wasn't teaching. She was known for always being available if anyone was in need.

Today, she had a heavy weight on her shoulders concerning Tilly. The phone call that Gillie had been dreading had come early that morning. The Housemother had been informed by a family friend,

Stephie, 'I'm afraid I've some bad news. Pete, Tilly's Dad, has asked me to contact you. Jo's not doing so well. Well, none of us are. The doctor hasn't given Jo much longer. It would be great if Tilly could come home.'

Gillie felt sick to the stomach and sat down in the nearest armchair for support. If she felt this bad, how was Tilly going to cope?

Stephie continued to pass on the information that Tilly needed to be able to travel home. 'Tell Tilly that her Dad will meet her at the station.'

Seventeen-year-old Tilly, one of her students, was well aware that the call was imminent. She had been in daily contact with her family. She could tell by the weakness in her Mum's voice, and the effort it took her to talk with any enthusiasm, that her Mum's strength was fast running out. Gillie admitted that it was one of the hardest things she'd had to do was to break the news to Tilly that it was time for her to go home.

After imparting the news to Tilly, she left the girl to pack after asking, 'Do you need any help?'

Over the last year, Tilly had demonstrated a reserve of strength which was deep and impenetrable. It was hard to breakthrough. Gillie had tried numerous times without any luck. Sometimes, she wished the girl would just break into tears. It would be easier. 'No, I'm fine. I'd rather be on my own,' she replied, 'but thanks anyway.'

Later that morning, when the occupants of Grantham House were all attending classes, Gillie accompanied Tilly along the corridor and down the two flights of stairs to the entrance hall. From start to finish, not one word was uttered. Gillie couldn't help but notice how tightly the girl was clutching onto her flute case. It was as though the black leather case containing the flute was the most important thing in the world. This tension from the vice-like grip was extending throughout Tilly's slim frame.

Gillie was deeply concerned. She knew she shouldn't have favourites but Tilly was something special. She had been a boarder at St C's since she was eleven years old, a gifted and talented student who had the world at her feet. She was now a seventeen year old with the worries of the world on her shoulders, so choked with emotion she was unable to speak and who was going home to spend whatever time was left with her beloved Mum.

To anyone who knew Tilly well, it was apparent that her Mum's illness had robbed the girl of her early teen years. She had walked through the illness with her Mum step by step, carrying a weight that had been far too heavy for a teen daughter to bear. The illness had stretched out over 5 years since the initial diagnosis. Throughout her time at the Academy, Tilly had been constantly on edge and had rung home every evening and sometimes during the day to check how her Mum was doing. Even when the news had been good, Tilly had never been able to relax. It was as though she had forgotten how to be a teen.

As Gillie said her goodbyes and helped Tilly to put her bags into the taxi that would take her to the station in the closest town, to catch the train home, she felt as though she wanted to hug the girl and take all the pain away and make it better. But nothing was going to make it better. It was only going to get worse and she felt a sense of helplessness. 'Let us know as soon as you arrive home. Give your Mum our love and tell her she is in our thoughts. Take care and keep in touch,' she offered as a parting gesture. She didn't know what else to say.

As she stood and watched the taxi disappear into the distance, she was overcome with a feeling of deep despair. She had met Tilly's Mum a few times at the Academy functions. She had been an adult version of Tilly, petite and delicate with those enormous eyes that spoke volumes. Tilly's parents had never missed a concert when Tilly was performing. They appeared to be a loving, supportive family. What would Tilly do without her beloved Mum? Only time would tell. 'Life's just not fair,' she said shaking her head as she made her way slowly up the two flights of stairs back to her flat.

Chapter 4

PETE HAD SUPPORTED HIS WIFE JO THROUGHOUT HER long illness. He had been a tower of strength, so brave, so encouraging and positive right up until the funeral. He had managed to deal with the final funeral arrangements calmly and logically.

The funeral service was held in the local church where the family had attended regularly until Jo had been too sick to be able to make the effort. From when Pete had walked into the kitchen that morning, he was understandably tense. Not once did he inquire as to how Tilly and Dan were bearing up. He appeared detached, acting more as though he was on auto-pilot. In the church, both Tilly and Dan were visibly distraught. They sat on either side of Stephie on the front pew taking comfort in her support as they both grappled with the proceedings and their consuming grief. In comparison, their Dad appeared to be devoid of emotion. He had failed to acknowledge any of the guests and had treated them as if they weren't there. Tilly noticed that people were staring with concern at his almost robotic behaviour. 'Yes, I'm fine,' he replied abruptly when people tried to offer their sympathy. 'No need to be concerned. Everything is OK.'

The reception for the guests was held at the family home as requested by Jo. She had previously made the arrangements with a caterer who supplied both the food and drink. Although it was August and still officially winter, the sun shone and the sky was blue. The house was full and so the patio doors had been opened to give the guests some well needed fresh air. One or two brave souls ignored the crisp air and wandered into the garden which had been Jo's pride and joy.

Later that afternoon, when all the guests except for Stephie, had left the house, Pete appeared to have completely lost it. Crumpling into a heap and retreating into his private grief, he kept anxiously pacing around the kitchen saying, 'This isn't happening. This can't be happening.'

Stephie, who was busy placing some of the leftover food in containers to be refrigerated for later use, noted his behaviour. Anxiously she said, 'Phone or text me anytime. I'm only just down the road. I can be here at a moment's notice. Don't feel as if you're being a nuisance. Nothing is too much trouble. Any time of the day or night, I can be here.'

'Off you go. We'll manage. We don't need you to call round now that Jo isn't here. Off you go,' he repeated briskly.

Knocked back by this sudden hostility, Stephie didn't know quite how to respond. Stunned, she pressed the lid down on the last container and swallowing hard, she managed, 'Well, if you're sure. It wouldn't be any trouble.'

She couldn't take his words in. Was this Pete talking to her? By the expression on his face, she knew he was serious. This wasn't the Pete she knew. She felt sick. Her stomach was in knots. She had just attended her best friend's funeral, as if that wasn't bad enough. She didn't know what to do, shout, cry or scream? She stood rooted to the spot.

'Off you go and don't bother coming back!' he shouted.

Just before she fled from the traumatic scene, she managed to whisper to Tilly and Dan, 'Text me.'

The shocked expressions on their faces said it all, 'We need you. Don't leave us to cope on our own.'

Stephie was in shock; she couldn't believe what had just happened. Quickly gathering up her belongings, she walked with head held high along the hallway in the direction of the front door and down the cobbled path to the front gate. She wasn't going to let Pete watch her humiliation. She tried to remain dignified as she rushed back down the tree-lined road to her home. She didn't want anyone to see her like this and she walked as quickly as she could without actually breaking into a run.

She was hurt to the core. It was as though a

bomb had dropped. She wanted to hide away in the security of her own home. She was unable to think of anything except how shell shocked she felt at that moment. Flinging open her front gate, she ran the last few steps up to the front door. By now, she didn't care what impression she was giving to the neighbours.

As she fumbled with her key, she started to shake violently and it took a few attempts for her to insert the key into the lock. The previous incident had given rise to emotions quite unlike her normal reactions. Her whole being was flooded with feelings of anger, betrayal, and rejection. Once in the sanctuary of her home, with no one to watch her reactions, she flung her bag down on the floor only just missing Dizzy who had run joyfully to meet her. The dog, taken aback by this behaviour, flattened her ears, dropped her tail and cowered in her bed in the corner, as her mistress screamed, stamped her feet and banged her fists on the wall until she couldn't tolerate the pain. 'How could he?' she yelled time after time.

Later that evening, after she'd broken down and cried her heart out for the first time since Jo had died, the events of the afternoon were analysed minute by minute. She wasn't stupid. She realised everyone was overwrought. Pete especially was at breaking point. The stress he'd held in check over the last five years must have been enormous. She hoped and prayed that he would seek professional grief counselling. If Pete had decided he didn't want her help, she decided it didn't matter. It was Dan and Tilly she was concerned about. She had promised Jo that she would be there for them and be there, she would.

Chapter 5

THE BANNING FROM VISITING THE FAMILY HOME, DIRECTED by Pete, had not just left Stephie's heart broken into tiny pieces; it had resulted in causing Dan and Tilly enormous stress. They were trying hard to cope with their grief, and on top of this, they were both devastated at their Dad's irrational outburst towards Stephie.

After they'd watched her uncomfortable departure, Dan said in disbelief, 'It's just not fair, not after all she's done for Mum.' He then stormed out of the kitchen. The next thing heard was the slamming of his bedroom door.

'I can't believe it,' whispered Tilly trying to hold back the tears. 'Dad, how could you be so cruel?'

However, one look at her Dad's thunderous expression told her to leave things as they were and not to make matters worse. It was completely out of character for him to be like this. Pete then took a hasty retreat into his study leaving Tilly alone with her thoughts. She realised her Dad was stressed out and suffering greatly but he shouldn't have spoken to Stephie like that. 'It's unforgivable,' she uttered under her breath. She knew he needed help but it was impossible to discuss anything with him. Now wasn't the time. He was like a bear with a sore head.

As if the incident involving Stephie wasn't bad enough, it wasn't long before Pete began an all-out war. He began by blaming the medical staff for Jo's death even though everyone was aware they had done a brilliant job. Nothing was right. He continued with a tirade against anyone who had anything to do with his wife's treatment.

Everyone knew Jo had received the very best care that had been on offer. They didn't need all of this ranting and raving. They were also aware that Pete wasn't a well man and needed some medical intervention but whatever they said was wrong. So, to avoid any form of confrontation, they stayed away and said nothing.

It was now left to Tilly to take on the responsibility of supporting Dan. It was a huge responsibility but Tilly had been through enough trauma herself. She couldn't take much more. She decided on an impulse, that for her sanity, she had to remove herself from the situation.

'I'm sorry; I've got lots of work to catch up on. I'm going to have to return to the Academy,' she explained to Dan.

Tilly's words were true but they weren't the only reason for her departure. She could have stayed at

home longer. She knew the Academy would understand and weren't expecting her to return quite so
soon after such an emotional event as her mother's
death. The truth was, the house held too many
reminders of happier times. The once busy, loving
home had now become a place of mourning and was
dysfunctional. Her Dad wasn't the Dad she knew and
loved. Dan appeared completely lost but was putting
a brave face on the situation. Everyone was trying to
come to terms with what had happened except they
were acting like robots, each with their own agenda.
The once complete happy family was now torn apart
and missing a vital piece of the jigsaw puzzle.

Two weeks after the funeral, Tilly made the brave
decision to pack her bags and return to the Academy.
She just couldn't stand the atmosphere at home any
longer. It was all too much. She asked Pete if he would
ring Gillie to inform her of her decision. The girl who
caught the train back to the Academy was fragile and
broken.

Chapter 6

IF ANYONE HAD ASKED GILLIE WHETHER TILLY WAS DOING the right thing in returning to the Academy so soon, she would have expressed great concern. She had been most surprised when Tilly's father had phoned her.

'Thought you'd like to know that Tilly will be returning to the Academy at the end of the week,' he stated.

'Oh!' was Gillie's immediate reaction. 'Isn't it rather soon? She's allowed more time you know?'

Pete replied devoid of any emotion, 'It's her decision. It will take her mind off things, keep her busy you know. We've all got to look to the future.' With that, he ended the call abruptly.

Gillie sighed, 'It's a bit odd,' she said to no one. 'Poor Tilly. I do hope she's OK.'

It was dark by the time the taxi arrived at the Academy. Thankfully, for Tilly, all the girls from Grantham House were in the dining room eating their evening meal. She couldn't have faced a reception committee. Gillie, who was expecting her stood outside her flat waiting. She watched Tilly pull her bags along the corridor towards her and felt such a rush of emotion. She wasn't a mother but every one of the girls in her care was treasured and her heart broke when she saw Tilly looking so pale, fragile and forlorn, a shadow of her former self. She speeded towards her with open arms and said with concern, 'Tilly, I'm so sorry, so sorry! Are you sure you're ready to return? You needn't have returned so soon, you know. We would have understood.'

Tilly had responded bravely with a definite, 'I'm fine, everything's fine.'

Gillie couldn't help but notice the determined expression on Tilly's thin face when she had spoken these words. She instinctively knew not to question her anymore or to ask after the rest of her family. She thought to herself, 'She's so brave. How terrible for her! She shouldn't be here. She needs time to grieve.'

She sensed it was too soon for the fiercely independent girl to open up to her and thought she'd watch and wait to see how things turned out. She ended the conversation with, 'You know where I am. My door is always open. It's great to see you back. Call in for a coffee anytime.' Gillie was well known for her coffee and chocolate cake.

Tilly knew the Housemother cared. There was no doubt about that. However, as the days went by, she felt that no one, not even Gillie had the remotest idea of the depth of her grief. What was especially hard was that no one mentioned her mum by name, not even Gillie. It was as though her wonderful, caring and fun-loving Mum had never existed. That was what hurt her deeply.

As the days went by, Tilly desperately yearned to chat about her mum. Everyone, even Amy, her best friend, appeared so self-conscious and uncomfortable when Tilly mentioned her mum. She'd noticed how they would look away and quickly change the subject. It was as though they were frightened in case it upset Tilly and brought on a flood of tears. That was what they feared. It wasn't that they didn't care. It was just that they hadn't personally experienced the death of a parent. They just didn't know how to respond. If they'd only realised, it would have done Tilly the world of good to have had a heartfelt sobbing session but they didn't.

The thing that upset and disappointed Tilly the most was Pete's inability to be able to talk to Tilly about his wife. When she spoke to him on the phone, he avoided the subject like the plague. She didn't want anything specific, just general chatter about Jo. Just things about what her mum had done and said. She had such a great need for this. Who could she talk to about the person she had loved more than she had loved herself?

On reflection, being at the Academy was much better than being at home. Tilly phoned home once a week, usually on a Sunday evening, when she knew her dad and Dan would most likely be available to chat. When her mum had been alive, she'd chatted whenever she felt like it but now it was different. She desperately needed this link with her home and the people who had been connected with Jo. According to the reports she received from Dan, her dad seemed to have nothing much to say to him. Pete had now become completely self-absorbed, depressed and appeared disinterested in everything. The only conversation he managed was to his clients at work. She was now used to the fact that if she required information it would be Dan she would be talking to.

Her brother usually filled her in about what was going on but he was also suffering in his way. 'I'm OK ... I suppose. I just wish that dad would talk to me, about Mum you know. He's taken all of her photos down except for the one of their wedding which he's still got in their room. He won't talk about her. He's like a robot. He comes home from work, asks me about school but I know he's not interested. We have dinner, and he spends the rest of the evening asleep in front of the TV or locked away in his study ... It's awful. I wish you were here.'

Tilly shared Dan's pain. 'I don't know what to say. Hang in there, I'll be home for Christmas,' she replied before cutting the call and dissolving into tears.

When she did manage a few words with her father, he answered any questions she might ask with a disinterested, 'Yes' or a 'No'. It was heartbreaking especially when she compared the chats she had shared with her mum. She would spill out all her news and Jo laughingly used to say, 'Slow down, I can't get a word in.'

The only other person Tilly would have talked to would have been Stephie but Pete had put a stop to that by telling her she wasn't wanted. That was something she couldn't forgive her dad for.

Tilly thought back to the easy-going, close-knit family she once had belonged to and felt the thread now left linking them together was taut enough to snap.

Chapter 7

Stephie heard the gate click. Dizzy, her beloved chocolate spaniel with the long, floppy ears didn't need to be told who the visitor was. As soon as she heard footsteps on the path she had bounded up onto the settee situated in front of the window and from where she had an excellent view of the road. The dog was, as usual, living up to her name. She had jumped off the settee with a huge leap before running up and down the hallway with tail and bottom wiggling frantically from side to side.

Stephie didn't need to be told who the visitor was. Dizzy only behaved with such excitement when one special person arrived. Stephie's prayers had been answered. She breathed a sigh of relief and shouted, 'Come on in. The doors unlocked.' To anyone else witnessing this scene, there would be nothing unusual. To Stephie, it meant the world.

Since the funeral, Stephie had spent hours analysing Pete's behaviour towards her. Of course, she understood he was grief-stricken. Pete had adored his wife.

They had been made for each other. However, she failed to understand why she had been banned from visiting the house where she had been welcomed for so many years. She still harboured his words deep in her heart and couldn't stop thinking of her promise to Jo that she would be there for Tilly and Dan. She had not had the nerve to pass by the house again. Perhaps this was taking the situation a little too seriously but Pete's behaviour towards her after the funeral was still so painful. So, Stephie had made sure that Dizzy was distracted when she left the house on her lead. She naturally tended to pull in the direction where her favourite people, Dan and Tilly lived. Weeks passed and Stephie's hopes of a reconciliation were wearing thin.

Dan stood outside on the doormat with head hung low and shoulders hunched with carrying around the weight of the world. Stephie was so relieved to see him, grasped his arm and led him down the hallway through to her kitchen at the back of the house. 'I didn't know whether I was allowed to come,' he spoke quietly almost a whisper.

'Of course, you can come, come as often as you like,' she blurted out, not knowing whether to laugh or cry.

'It was after what Dad said,' he looked at her with such pity in his eyes.

'Your dad said I wasn't to call at your house, but I can't remember him saying you couldn't visit me, did he?' she asked hoping the answer would be in the negative.

'No, he didn't say anything,' Dan said with the first hint of a smile.

'It's time for Dizzy to go for a walk, how about you come with us? I know Dizzy would be thrilled. She's missed you,' she said thinking of how the dog had spent hours waiting at the front gate gazing up the road for a glimpse of Dan. This had upset her more than she could ever explain to the boy.

The official 'Dog Park' had originally been a nine-hole golf course that had been decommissioned. It was a wonderful place where dogs could legally be let off their leads and run freely. There were different routes you could take. There were open areas, where the fairways had been. These were great for throwing a ball and gave the dogs plenty of scope for running to retrieve their favourite toys. In the rough areas to the side, were the stands of native eucalyptus trees giving shade when the sun was at its highest.

Dizzy absolutely loved the park which was a five minute drive away from where Stephie lived. It served a double purpose as not only was it therapeutic for the dogs, it was also a meeting place for their owners. It depended on the time of day or how hot it was. The best time to catch up for a chat was late afternoon/ early evening in summer. People would often tag along and chat as they walked their dogs. Mostly the conversations were about the dogs.

Since Jo had died, Stephie had been at her lowest ebb. She had taken to walking Dizzy when the park was quieter as she hadn't always felt like talking or answering the many inquires she had received following Jo's death. However, on this occasion, now that Dan had decided to join her, she sensed he wanted to talk about his mum and as it was after school time and tending to be busier, they had chosen the less popular route.

At first, Dan was hesitant. He hadn't spoken to Stephie since the awful day of the funeral and it was now approaching Christmas. She could feel his awkwardness. He was no longer the little boy who would chat non-stop. She didn't push him. She didn't prod. She left it up to him. Eventually, Dizzy worked her magic on him. Perhaps it was the subtle way she ran up to him and dropped the ball at his feet. If there was no response, she resorted to nudging his hand with her wet nose. After a few attempts, he just couldn't refuse. She had such an exuberant way of making everything so exciting, and on this occasion, she was even livelier than ever as she was so thrilled to have her friend back in the park with her. Stephie watched Dan begin to thaw and breathed a sigh of relief. It wasn't long before he was confiding in her. Once he started, he couldn't stop.

'Oh Stephie, it's just awful. I know it'll never be the same but I never thought it would be this bad.' He shuffled his feet in the red pea gravel and Stephie noticed his sneakers were covered in red dust. The stupid things you notice, she thought to herself. Dan's head hung low. His shoulders were hunched and she could feel the tension emanating from his body.

'How's your father?' she asked hesitantly.

'He hardly ever speaks, only when he has to, you know. He's begun to do a lot of his work from home now. I don't think he's handling any of it well. He sounds OK when he talks to his clients on the phone but he never asks me how I'm doing. I don't think he cares about anything now that Mum's gone.'

Stephie pondered his words before speaking. Dizzy had been racing around at top speed but she seemed to sense something was wrong and came to sit in front of Dan, who had by now, stopped throwing the ball. It sounds as though your dad needs some grief counselling.'

'He won't go.'

'What about you? You can't shoulder all of this on top of your schoolwork.'

'It's not so bad at school as the work is full-on and it helps me to think of other things. I've had a few chats with the counsellor at school. I also talk to Tilly once a week. I wish she wasn't so far away. You know, Dad has removed all the photos in the house with Mum on.'

'Oh no, that's awful!' responded Stephie with shock. Jo had been Pete's first and only love. Their home had been a testament to their love. Photos from the time they'd first met, of their wedding and then later of the family had adorned the walls, shelves, and tables. This was serious.

'Well, he's left one of their wedding photos in their bedroom.'

'I just can't believe it.' She thought of how Jo would have reacted if she'd known. Tentatively, she asked, 'How is Tilly?' She instantly felt guilty that she hadn't been in contact with her. It wasn't that she hadn't wanted to. She blamed it on the situation with Pete. She hadn't wanted to overstep the mark. He had made it quite plain that she was not welcome and although Tilly was not living at the family home, she had felt wary about being in contact with any of the family.

'She phones mostly on a Sunday evening. She's not the same. I miss her,' he said trying to subdue his emotions.

'It's OK to miss people you know,' she said. 'I miss your Mum dreadfully.'

Immediately, Stephie regretted her words as Dan abruptly turned away with his head bent. She watched him with concern, her heart beating fast as he walked away from her towards some trees at the side of the old fairway. However, looking down at Dizzy, who was staring at Dan's back with such a look of despair on her face, Stephie was hit by a strange feeling. She couldn't explain it. She watched in wonderment as Dizzy, tail dropped low, slowly and silently, followed Dan. Stephie knew that he needed time alone so she walked to a nearby tree where she could watch without being seen. She felt the tears sliding down her face as she watched Dan sitting on the ground clasping onto Dizzy as though they were the only two left in a sinking ship. Dizzy was busily licking Dan's face. It was as though she wanted to make sure there were no tears left. Since Jo's death, it was the most beautiful moment she had witnessed and a definite turning point, not just for Dan and the dog, but for her as well.

It was at that moment when an idea sprung into her mind. 'I won't mention anything at the moment,' she thought to herself. 'It's too early.'

Chapter 8

Gillie sighed heavily, as she entered her flat having just spoken to Tilly. She was very fond of the girl but admitted she found her evasive on occasions. You never really knew what was going on in her mind. This had become more evident since her recent return. She gave the impression that all was fine, but the Housemother sensed otherwise. It was as though she had an inner reserve of strength that was impenetrable. The Housemother realised how little she'd actually seen Tilly since her return and immediately was overcome with guilt.

The conversation had run something along these lines, 'How are you, Tilly?'

'I'm fine, thanks.'

'Have you time for a hot chocolate?' This was a drink she knew would normally grab the attention of any of the girls on the corridor.'

'Thanks, but not this time. I've too much to do.'

'Well, perhaps next time. Don't work too hard.'

'No, I won't,' replied Tilly as she scuttled along the corridor to her room.

Tilly hadn't fooled her Housemother for a second with her continued affirmations that she felt fine and all was well. You only had to look at the girl. There was no need for words. Tilly was even thinner and more drawn than ever, and this was a real cause for concern.

Tilly had returned to the Academy feeling a wreck. She was seventeen. All the vibrancy of youth had died when she had lost her Mum. She was drained of all emotion. She was empty. There was nothing left. Life was just too difficult.

Throughout her mum's long and difficult illness, Tilly had chatted regularly with her on the phone or via Skype. She missed those chats more than anything. She used to close her door, curl up on her bed and just talk, talk that went on for hours. It probably wasn't hours but it seemed like mother and daughter would have spent hours discussing anything and everything. It was amazing how much they could talk about. When she wasn't talking, she was texting.

Being at the Academy wasn't the same anymore. She was surrounded by small things, incidents so insignificant to others but which had a huge impact on her. She couldn't stop the other girls from phoning their mums but it hurt her to the core when she heard them on the phone. She couldn't explain how desperate she was to talk to her mum. It was killing her inside. 'Oh Mum, I miss you like crazy,' she would utter under her breath.

Worse of all, was that Tilly felt completely isolated. She couldn't even talk to her friend Amy anymore. No one understood how she felt. How could they? They were not her. It was so bad that in the privacy of her room, she'd taken to listening to her mum's old messages which she'd left on her phone. Whilst she could still hear her voice, part of Jo was still alive.

In the past, she had dialed her mum's mobile just so she could hear, 'Hi, you've reached Jo. Leave a message and I'll get back to you.'

'Mum, I'm missing you to the moon and back,' was Tilly's last reply before the phone had been de-registered. Had any of this helped? Tilly was not so sure. Instead, she said out loud, 'I can't wrap my head around this anymore. I think I'm going mad.'

There were so many emotions crowding her body, swirling around and sucking her dry of any positive feelings. It was just too much. Tilly wondered if she would ever feel normal again. It had seemed such an age, so long she could hardly remember when her life had been what other people would have called normal. Was there such a thing as a normal life? Perhaps less stressful would be a better description. She felt as though her life had been nothing but stressful, not just since she had lost her mum but throughout all the treatments Jo had undergone. There had always been something to worry about and towards the end, the fear of losing her Mum.

As time went on, Tilly was still very emotional, the outbursts of grief hitting her suddenly when she was least expecting it. At times, she could function normally and then something would happen that would jolt her back to the painful times she thought she had stored away forever in her memory. However, she was beginning to realise that they lingered just below the surface, never far away. No one saw this side of Tilly. She hid her emotions well. No one witnessed the occasions when she was reduced to a sobbing mess.

One thing to be thankful for was that the Academy ran such a hectic schedule. What with lessons, rehearsals for concerts and her private flute lessons with her favourite teacher, Mr Ford, there was less time to dwell on her problems. However, even though she was busy, there was not a day in which Tilly didn't think about her mum.

Most of her spare time outside of classes had been taken up with rehearsals for the Christmas Concert. The excitement was high amongst the students. There was a definite buzz in the air as they rehearsed for the final concert of the year, a huge affair which was attended by parents as well as talent scouts and musical directors. It was a ticketed event and there was always a rush to purchase tickets which sold out quickly.

For Tilly, this image of glitz and glamour in which all the girls had their hair and make-up done before stepping into their long royal blue shimmery dresses adorned with their personalised purple silk flowers, pulled her down rather than elevated her spirits. It was the first time she had no family attending, no one who belonged to her to boost her confidence by complimenting her on her performance. Every musician needed that. She couldn't forgive her dad the last time she had spoken to him. She had felt so disappointed and let down when she had mentioned the concert. 'Don't expect me to attend this year. I can't. I just can't.'

'But Dad, you always come,' she'd pleaded.

'Well, I can't come this year,' he'd replied bluntly.

'Please, Dad. You and Mum have always come,' her voice was rising and becoming more urgent.

'Well, I can't come this year.'

'Why not? Mum would have come if she'd been here,' she implored.

There was a silence at the end of the phone. She thought she heard a gasp or was it a sob? She waited. The silence continued. She couldn't believe it. He'd hung up on her.

Tilly felt as if he had stabbed her in her heart. She couldn't explain it in any other words. It had been a bitter blow more so as everyone else's parents were planning to attend. She was so disappointed that he had felt he couldn't make the effort. Surely he knew how important it was to her for the family, or what was left of it, to be present to hear her play her solo? It also meant that if he couldn't attend, Dan wouldn't be there either.

Her dad had, this year, decided he was unable to attend. It was another blow. The fact of his decision not to attend the concert was doing her head in. She couldn't remember a time before when her parents had not made the effort to travel to the Academy for a major concert.

Feeling rejected and so alone, Tilly set off for one of her frequent bushwalks in which she found solace. She did not need to sign herself out; the Academy grounds were extensive enough for her to make her escape. There was no one around on the many bush tracks. It was where she could rationalise events. On this occasion, she walked and waited for a call that didn't come. She hoped her dad would have second thoughts, realise how important his presence at the concert was to her. However, there was no follow up explanation. No apologies. No, 'I hope you'll do well. I wish I could be there to listen to your solo.'

Chapter 9

Gillie could not help but notice Tilly's crestfallen face during the lead up to the concert. However, she felt powerless to help. Whenever she had tried to approach Tilly to offer any assistance, her requests had fallen on deaf ears and she was rewarded for her efforts with, 'I'm fine. Everything's fine.'

She had, on numerous occasions since Tilly's return to the Academy, suggested Tilly see a grief counsellor. The reply, as usual, had been greeted with stoicism, a head held high followed by, her stock reply, 'I'm fine. I don't need any help.'

It was obvious to everyone that Tilly was not in a good place. Other members of staff were continually commenting that she had lost her spark, that she wasn't the girl she used to be and so on. However, no one could find fault with her academic work or music studies. Jack Ford, the flute tutor, was dispirited. Tilly was still playing well. He couldn't fault her. However, she appeared too serious and tense. Of course, he could understand why.

Gillie had at last decided to take matters into her own hands. Having positioned herself by a window, she had watched Amy walk towards Grantham House from the Music Block. At one stage, Amy and Tilly had been inseparable. They had begun studying at the Academy at the same time. Both girls were intense about their music studies. Amy was a brilliant violinist who played with a passion not normally seen in such a young girl. However, since Tilly had returned to the Academy following the death of her mum, she appeared to have distanced herself from everyone, including Amy and was frequently seen alone.

The Housemother, who had been at her wit's end as to what to do about Tilly's state of mind had conveniently located herself at the top of the staircase where she knew Amy would have to pass to reach her room. 'Come and have a coffee with me. It's ages since I've seen you,' she said to the surprised Amy.

It was quite a common occurrence for Gillie to chat over coffee, but the expression on Amy's face told Gillie that the girl was apprehensive. 'Don't worry, there's nothing wrong. Well, not with you,' she'd replied, to put Amy at ease.

When Amy walked into the flat, she said immediately, 'It's about Tilly isn't it?'

'Well, yes it is. Please make yourself comfy. Would you like a drink, hot chocolate perhaps?' Gillie knew that most girls began to relax once they had a drink and a piece of her special home-baked chocolate cake in front of them. 'You used to spend all your free time hanging out with Tilly but I haven't noticed you around together much recently. Is everything OK?'

Amy pushed the chocolate cake around the plate with her fork. She refused to look Gillie in the eye and after a pause replied, 'It's just that she's changed so much since her Mum died. She doesn't want to go anywhere or do the things we used to do. I can't talk to her anymore. She's just not interested. We used to have so much fun. Now, she's so serious about everything.'

Gillie nodded her head. 'I understand,' she replied. 'Have you talked to her about her mum?'

Amy fidgeted on the settee, looked up guiltily and shook her head. 'No. I don't know what to say to her. I don't know how to talk to her. We all feel the same. We're scared of what she may do if we mention her mum or talk about our mums.'

Gillie waited a moment before responding, 'I know it's not easy but I'd like you to try. She's going through an awful stage. All girls need their mums. Even if sometimes you don't think you do. Christmas is coming and it's going to be very hard for her and her family. Don't dwell on things but just try to talk normally and include her in. Give it a try, please.'

Amy replied by nodding her head. However, it wasn't going to be easy.

Chapter 10

Little did the Housemother know how bad things were for Tilly. Christmas was a huge affair in the lives of the students at St C's. Tilly had begun to dread walking across to Franklin House where the academic lessons were held. The building had once been a beautiful historic home built in the early 1800s. It was originally owned by a wealthy, business family named Humphrey-Bond. It wasn't the building that spooked Tilly but the huge Christmas tree which had been installed as usual on 1st December. It was situated in the enormous entrance hall and was heavily decorated with sparkling lights, baubles, and bows. The Academy wasn't known for squandering its funds. Every year there was always the huge spruce tree. It was a beautiful sight. This year the theme was based on a European Christmas and the tree was festooned in white and sparkling silver with a hint of ruby red.

Just the thoughts of the festive season made Tilly feel physically sick. She associated Christmas with her home. As far back as she could remember Jo had always delighted in making such an effort with the decorations and food. This year it wouldn't be the same. It could never be the same again, ever. In her last conversation with her brother, she had gleaned that if things were left to her dad, there wouldn't be a Christmas at their house at all.

Tilly desperately wished that Christmas could be cancelled this year. Every time she heard the choir rehearsing carols for the many carol services at which they performed, it rubbed it in even deeper. Didn't they know how she was feeling? Usually so quietly confident, when she performed on stage, this year saw her fighting to hide her tears. She only just managed to get through the Christmas concert. However, there were harder things to face, one being the highlight of the Academy's social calendar, the Christmas Ball, a glittering affair.

Normally, she would have been as excited as everyone else but not this year. This year she was dreading it. She had taken to disappearing into her room straight after dinner. She told everyone she was going to practise her flute but everyone knew this wasn't true. No musical sounds were coming from her room.

Tilly often featured as a topic for gossip amongst the girls. What they didn't know, they made up. This evening, after Amy's chat with Gillie, Amy felt the weight of her conversation hanging heavily on her shoulders. Jessica piped up as normal, 'Thank God

Tilly's not here. She's such a party pooper. I know she's lost her mum and that's terrible but we don't all have to suffer with her do we?'

Amy had looked uncomfortable and staring down at her feet had replied, 'Well, we could try and include her in. It's not easy for her.'

'Well, you've changed your mind. Last week you agreed that you had had enough and didn't want her as a friend anymore. You can go and keep her company,' replied Jessica. 'She makes us feel guilty if we enjoy ourselves.'

Amy bit her tongue and looked as though she wished the ground would swallow her up. 'Well, she needs someone,' replied Amy as she turned her back on the group and headed up the corridor in the direction of Tilly's room.

Tilly had no idea how her behaviour was affecting everyone else. She was so depressed she could only concentrate on herself. She knew she needed help but was unaware of just how desperate her situation was. Gillie had mentioned grief counselling to her but she didn't feel she was ready. In truth, she didn't believe anyone would be able to help her, not even a professional person could have an understanding of how she felt. The thoughts of sitting opposite a stranger and baring her innermost thoughts and feelings were too personal for Tilly. It had never entered her head that talking to a stranger may be easier than talking to someone you knew.

It didn't take Tilly long to decide she wasn't going to attend the Christmas Ball this year. She was sick of hearing about it. She had no interest in choosing a long formal dress and getting her hair and nails done. She kept her thoughts about attending the ball to herself. No one asked if she was going, what she was wearing or who was taking her. This suited Tilly. However, at the same time, it was almost as if she had been erased from the scene. She felt as though she had become invisible. To be honest, she didn't want to go, but deep down it would have been nice to have been included. It cut her to the core, especially when she overheard Jessica saying loudly, 'Well, it's no good asking her. If she came, she'd only spoil it for the rest of us. No guy would want to take her with her sour face.'

On every floor in Grantham House, the latest magazines were scoured and the gossip columns on social media were followed intensely to see what their favourite pop stars and film stars were wearing. Some lucky girls like Amanda, whose mother ran a chain of fashion boutiques, had their dresses designed especially for them. Other girls, who were not as lucky as Amanda, persuaded their parents to transfer money into their bank accounts so they could travel into the city to purchase their dresses. There was a lot of competition amongst the girls as to who was going to be 'hot'. Even the boys made an effort to brush up as they were expected to arrive in smart suits or formal dinner jackets with bow ties. The Academy had set high standards that had to be followed.

Tilly had tried to opt-out of attending and had made every excuse she could think of to get out of going. 'I haven't got a partner or a new dress. I'll feel awkward,' were her initial responses to the adamant Housemother.

However, Gillie had put her foot down with the words, 'No, you are not spending the evening locked away in your room. Making the effort to get dressed up; you'll feel a new person. It'll do you good.'

'Please don't make me go,' she pleaded almost on the verge of tears.

Gillie felt like a monster. She wasn't comfortable taking this stance but she felt it wasn't going to be good for Tilly in the long run if she allowed her to continue her hermit existence.

Surprisingly, Amy had stepped in to help her choose her dress. Tilly was sure that Gillie had something to do with this but kept her thoughts to herself. Even though Tilly was appreciative of Amy's efforts, the act in itself accentuated the fact that for the very first time, her mum wasn't around to help her choose a dress. The two girls had caught the bus into the city on the Saturday afternoon before the ball. Tilly wasn't a bundle of fun but she'd tried to enter into the spirit of the event. They'd scoured the shops and just as Tilly was about to say, 'I can't find anything I like so I won't be able to go.' Amy, in desperation, suggested a small boutique situated close to the bus stop.

'Come on, just have a look.'

'OK, but I doubt I'll find anything,' replied a reluctant Tilly as Amy grabbed her hand and pulled her into the tiny boutique.

It was filled with ball gowns and the assistant was determined she was going to make a sale that afternoon. Tilly was virtually forced into trying on gown after gown. Because she had lost so much weight, she looked model-like in all of them. Due to her reluctance in choosing a gown, it was left to Amy and the assistant to make the final choice. It was a floaty floral chiffon number in shades of gold and rusts. With Tilly's auburn tints and hazel eyes and with hair and makeup done, she'd look a 'million dollars'.

In exasperation, Amy declared, 'That's the one! Please wrap it, we have a bus to catch,' before hurling Tilly out of the shop towards the bus stop. Poor Amy felt she deserved a medal after such an arduous afternoon. She wished she could do something to cheer up her friend. At the moment, it appeared a thankless exercise.

Tilly had attended the Ball under sufferance. She looked fantastic but that did nothing to raise her spirits. The Ball was held as usual in the original ballroom of Franklin House. It was a beautiful room and had been decorated with mini trees in terracotta pots, which were showered with tiny twinkling lights. The colour scheme was white and silver and matched the huge Christmas tree in the entrance hall. The buffet supper was spread out on tables arranged on each side of the room. The table-cloths and decorations were in ruby red, adding to the Christmas scene. Under any other circumstance, Tilly would have been enrapt with the sight and the atmosphere it created.

For most of the evening she had forced a smile on her face that was so artificial that by the end of the evening, her face physically hurt. Amy had tried her best to drag her onto the dance floor. Tilly noticed the expressions on the faces of the group dancing together. They didn't have to say anything. She knew they didn't want her there spoiling their fun. She had found an unoccupied table where she sat for the remainder of the evening. Her body language said it all and so she was left alone with her memories.

Thoughts circled round and round inside her head. Memories could be kind. Memories could be cruel. It didn't matter what Tilly did, the pictures surfacing from her inner depths wouldn't leave her in peace. Before the night of the ball, she'd tried keeping busy, keeping her mind focussed on anything but Christmas. How could she not forget Christmas when every-where there was evidence of it? The sparkling silver, the purity of the white and the richness of the ruby red swirled around inside her head. She felt haunted.

She thought of last year when her mum had been alive. She hadn't gone with Tilly to choose a dress as she had been too sick. However, they'd scoured the internet together and Jo had made a few suggestions. With these in mind, Tilly had then gone into the city and had tried on a selection of the dresses. At least with the aid of Skype, mother and daughter had been able to share the experience.

This year it was so hard. There was this gaping hole inside her and she couldn't explain it to anyone. She felt so alone in her pain. She couldn't forgive her dad for banishing Stephie from visiting the family. Her thoughts drifted to think of Stephie. Deep down she wanted to see Stephie, but she'd not been in contact with Tilly, She'd not only lost her mum. Through the actions of Pete, she'd lost Stephie who was the next best thing. She wondered why Stephie hadn't been in touch. She felt betrayed and abandoned.

When Tilly thought hard about last Christmas, it hadn't been so great. Jo had been ill, but not so ill that she couldn't join in the festivities. Thinking back, Tilly likened the occasion to a play where everyone was an actor who had their part to play but understood that it wasn't real and that everything had been staged. Everyone was too polite. The conversation was stilted. Sentences started but weren't completed and no questions were asked. Normally there would have been references to the New Year, discussions about holiday plans, etc, but not last year. If she was truthful, she had dreaded that particular Christmas. She was sick of people telling her she would eventually forget the awful, painful memories and all she would remember would be the good times. She hadn't managed to reach that stage yet. Most of her thoughts dwelt on how much she missed her mum and how much she physically ached to talk to her.

Chapter 11

What a Christmas this one had turned out to be!

Pete had met Tilly at the station; there was no warm, welcoming kiss on the cheek. After a luke-warm hug and an even cooler, 'Good to see you,' he'd driven her home. There was no, 'I've really missed you. It's great that you're here. How did the concert go? Did you enjoy the Ball?' She felt abandoned by his rejection. It was obvious that Pete didn't seem interested in her anymore. This was a bitter pill to swallow. When she had tried to engage him in conversation, all she'd received was a disinterested grunt. She turned her head right to look at him and noticed his cool exterior. She wanted to scream.

When they arrived at the house, she didn't call it home anymore, her fears were justified. Her dad parked the car in the drive. Her heart dropped to the pit of her stomach or that's how it felt. The garden, her mum's pride and joy! What was left of the lawn was brown and burnt. It was obvious no one had watered it. The flowers in the border around the lawn had suffered a similar fate. They were all shrivelled up and were also brown. The old wheelbarrow filled with blooms had fared slightly better probably as the petunias could cope with the hot summer sun. Perhaps because they were close to the front door, it hadn't been such an effort to water them. What would her mum have thought?

Dan had warned her that things were bad. If this was outside, what was she going to find inside? The emotions she felt on entering the hall, cut through her like a knife and left her feeling incomplete, cold and emotionless. No tree with twinkling lights to greet her. No gifts wrapped and labelled under the tree.

Pete, her Dad, was totally out of it. Every piece of furniture was covered in dust. Cards, still unopened lay in a heap on the hall table by the front door. Tilly knew it would be different this year but hadn't anticipated how far things had deteriorated. Her mum, Jo, had always enjoyed Christmas. She'd spent ages preparing for the event, often starting her shopping for gifts in the July sales. Tilly didn't expect the same from her Dad, but this was awful. It was numbing. Without her mum, there would be no Christmas cake or mince pies in airtight tins in the pantry. No food prepared. Nothing!

Even though she had initially shrugged her shoulders at going to the Ball and all the other Christmas festivities at the Academy, all the activity had kept her mind occupied and had shielded her away from the real world. Now she was forced to face reality. However, she had not been prepared for this. It was such a contrast from the Academy Tilly had just left.

Tilly dumped her case in the hall, thinking of how her mum would have said, 'Tilly, take your case up to your room. We don't want to make the place untidy.' It couldn't make it appear any more of a mess than it was.

At least Dan was pleased to see her. He greeted his sister with a great big hug. 'Thank God, you're home. It's been a nightmare here,' he whispered so that his dad couldn't hear him. He needn't have bothered. His father was already closeted in his office with the door tightly shut.

Tilly was unable to speak. She looked at her brother, hunched her shoulders and stared around her as if to question what was going on. Dan shrugged his shoulders in reply. 'Come for a walk with me. I can't talk here,' he said.

The weather was warm. They just set off with nowhere in particular in mind. Dan couldn't stop talking. It was as though he'd not talked to anyone for so long. Even though he'd spoken to his sister on the phone and sent messages via Instagram, it still wasn't like talking face to face. All his emotions had been bottled up and now they were overflowing. 'It's been awful here since Mum went. Dad has changed so much. He just works and sleeps. He doesn't even seem bothered whether he eats most of the time. He doesn't talk to me unless he has to. The house is a tip. He doesn't care. Mum would be appalled if she could see how things are.'

'Yes, I can see what you mean,' Tilly sighed deeply. 'I know you said it was bad, but I didn't expect it to be as bad as it is. It's been hard for me too,' responded Tilly, 'I miss Mum so much.'

A few steps later, Tilly continued, 'I don't know how you've managed to cope. I'll never forgive Dad for banning Stephie from the house. She could have helped us so much.'

'It's not been easy. The school's been very supportive and some of the guys' parents have invited me round for meals. There's something else but you mustn't tell Dad,' he said looking uncomfortable.

'What is it? Tell me.'

'I've been down to Stephie's house a couple of times after school. She's great. We've taken Dizzy out to the park. It's helped.'

'But why didn't you tell me? Why didn't Stephie phone me? I would have given anything to have talked to her. I've needed her so much.'

'Til,' he replied, referring to her by the name he used when Matilda seemed too long and difficult, 'it's only been during the last two weeks and I was going to tell you when you arrived home. Please don't get cross. She told me she's wanted to contact you but she hesitated over it. Dad really upset her when he told her she wasn't needed. She didn't want to get us into trouble.'

Dan could see how much his sister was hurting. The tears she was trying to hide, how her arms were wrapped protectively around the front of her body and how she stomped ahead of him. He quickened his steps to keep up with her.

'Til, don't take it out on me. I was going to tell you.'

'I hope you're telling the truth.'

'You know I am. Don't fall out with me. I couldn't cope without you,' he pleaded. 'Let's go and get a cool drink.'

Later sitting outside the cafe under an umbrella, she realised she'd overreacted. She hated to admit it but she was envious of her brother. She desperately needed contact with Stephie just as much as Dan did. Stephie had been Jo's best friend. If she couldn't have her mum, Stephie came a close second.

She couldn't blame Stephie. It was true that she hadn't made any effort to keep in touch. Her Dad had made it quite clear Stephie was to leave the family alone. Perhaps Stephie was doing what she thought was the best thing. When Tilly had looked at the neglect in the house and thought about how her dad had taken himself off to his office almost as soon as she'd arrived home, she realised that the situation was serious. She knew that if she'd been the one who had been left at home, she would have acted in the same way and would have visited Stephie straight away.

Tilly's first night at home had been restless. Her bedroom was covered in dust and the sheets appeared to be the same crumpled ones that had been on the bed when she had returned to the Academy after the funeral. 'This is awful. What are we going to do?' she muttered to herself.

The next morning, Tilly and Dan were woken out of their despondency by the front doorbell which was emitting a piercing rendition of, 'There's a Welcome in the Highlands', a Scottish song which was totally out of place in Australia and, for some reason, had always made their mum laugh. This particular morning, there was no frivolity and the tinny sound rang out in stark contrast to the preceding silence.

When Tilly opened the door, she was hesitant to respond to Stephie who was apprehensively standing on the doormat. When she quickly realised, that the visitor was as nervous as she was herself, she flung herself into the arms of Stephie, who responded by wrapping her arms tightly around the thin, pale young woman in response and held them in place until Tilly's tear wrenching-sobs had almost come to a halt.

Dan had quickly followed his sister to the door and had witnessed the emotional outburst. When there was a lull, Stephie said quietly, 'Hi there, you two. If you don't stop Tilly, you'll have me in tears as well and I don't want to ruin my makeup. Is your father in?'

When there was a nodding of heads in unison, she whispered, 'Come on down to my place. Come and say hello to Dizzy.'

As they nodded their heads in unison, they quietly closed the door behind them and followed Stephie down the path. Further down the road, she suggested, 'Perhaps you'd both like to go for a walk in the park?'

Dan draped his arm around his sister's shoulders, looked at her and mouthed, 'Are you OK?'

When she nodded, he turned to Stephie and said with a huge grin spreading from ear to ear, 'That'd be cool. We're both fine with that.'

Chapter 12

PETE HAD MADE NO EFFORT TO CELEBRATE THIS FIRST festive season without his dearly loved wife. If it had been left up to him, Christmas would have gone by without any reference to the festive season. However, Tilly and her brother had other ideas. They dashed around the shops to buy presents and food and speedily put up the tree. Sitting on the floor unwrapping the glass baubles from the box, where Jo had carefully placed them the previous year, was harder than either of them imagined. Each glittering decoration was a story in itself. 'Can you remember when Mum bought this one?' asked Tilly holding up a red glass maple leaf edged with gold.

'Don't think so,' replied Dan.

'It was when we were on holiday in Canada and we visited the Christmas Shop in Banff that was open all year.'

'Oh yes,' said Dan. 'That was when Mum was well. I wish she was here now,' he said with a tremble in his voice.

'So do I. I miss her so much,' Tilly managed to say before bursting into tears ... and that's how the afternoon progressed, tears, followed by stories of happier times and then more tears. Even though Tilly and Dan were unaware, the actions were therapeutic and were the beginnings of working through their grief. It was unfortunate for Pete that he felt unable to join in and scathingly said, 'I don't know why you're bothering. I don't want to look at that tree.'

'We're doing it for Mum and us. It's what she would have wanted.'

Pete grabbed his car keys from the hall table and headed for the front door. The last they heard from him that evening was the screech of the car tyres on the gravel.

Thankfully, later that evening Stephie had bravely arrived at the front door, unannounced for a second time. Earlier that day she had decided she needed to make contact with Tilly and Dan again to honour the promise she had made to Jo that she would be there for them. Not wanting to cause upsets or have Tilly and Dan subjected to a barrage of hurtful comments thrown at them from their father in one of his frequent rages, she had positioned herself at her gate with Dizzy, waiting for an opportunity. She had not had to stand there long before she had witnessed Pete's rapid exit from the family home. 'What's happened now?' she whispered out loud.

It wasn't long before arriving and being dragged

into the house by Tilly and Dan that Stephie heard about the trauma that had driven Pete to leave in such a hurry. 'Oh, my poor darlings,' said Stephie trying to curb her emotions. 'You shouldn't have to go through all of this stress especially after all that's happened. I just wish your dad would agree to have some counselling or at least talk to someone. Anyway, I came to ask you to join me for dinner at my house on Christmas Day. You don't want the bother of having to prepare a meal and I'd love you to come.'

'Oh, that would be wonderful!' they both replied together. Tilly continued with a frown, 'But what about Dad? It is Christmas after all. We can't leave him on his own.'

'Yes, we can,' stated Dan with a determined expression written across his face that Stephie had never witnessed before. 'He said he doesn't want to celebrate Christmas. He can stay here. He'll only ruin it for everybody else.'

'No, no,' replied Stephie. 'Of course, he's invited. It's only right. It's up to him to decide whether he comes. The last thing I want is more upset.'

However, when Stephie's visit was mentioned to Pete, followed by the invite for him to be included in the festivities, he didn't show much enthusiasm. 'I thought I'd told that woman to keep away,' he answered rudely.

'Well, we're going,' replied Tilly and Dan in unison. 'It's not going to be much fun staying in this house and don't call Stephie, *that woman*. It's unkind and Mum wouldn't like to hear you call her that. If you don't want to come, that's fine with us.'

Tilly marched towards the door, turned with a fierce expression on her face and said, 'Mum would be really disappointed if you refused to come.' With that, they both marched out of the house in the direction of Stephie's.

After a lot of thought and soul searching, Pete had reluctantly agreed to attend. He would never admit it but Tilly's words had stung him and had made him face reality for a short time. However, this was short-lived. He had dragged himself to Stephie's but to everyone's disappointment, he had been unable to lift himself out of his misery and had made no effort to enter into the Christmas spirit. It was as though he was there in body but not in spirit and his heart certainly wasn't in it.

When the atmosphere became almost unbearable, Stephie had suggested taking Dizzy for a walk in the park. 'I don't know about anyone else, but I feel stuffed! How about a walk in the park?'

Tilly and Dan breathed a sigh of relief. When Dizzy heard the word 'walk', she was raring to go even if her little tummy was full to the brim with turkey and the trimmings. It was the only day Stephie gave in and allowed the dog to eat the same food as her guests. She did, however, draw the line at sharing her Christmas pudding with the dog.

It was as they moved towards the front door, Pete stood up and said, 'Thanks for the meal. Think I'll give the dog walking a miss.' With that, he left to go home and everyone began to relax.

When it came to the New Year, Tilly and Dan collected a Chinese takeaway, downloaded some movies and tried to forget it was supposed to be a new start to a New Year. Deep in their hearts, they both wanted to return to a previous time when their mum had been alive, not go hurtling into a future of unknown emptiness.

The remainder of the festive break was a blur of cleaning, washing and generally trying to improve the appearance of the house. It was done for Dan. Tilly felt an obligation to improve her brother's existence in a house that wasn't a home anymore.

Before Tilly stepped out of the car at the station on her way back to the Academy, she tentatively said to her Dad, 'Dan and I are really worried about you. Do you think it might be a good idea to go to see the Doctor?'

Pete, obviously rather taken aback by this, shrugged his shoulders before replying harshly, 'No, there's nothing wrong with me.'

However, on the drive home from the station, his sight became blurry. He was shedding the first tears since his wife had died. Tilly's words had affected him more than he'd like to admit.

Chapter 13

IT WAS NOT SURPRISING THAT AFTER CHRISTMAS, TILLY had returned to the Academy for her final year in very low spirits. She was in a state of limbo. She had none of her earlier enthusiasm for her studies. She didn't want to be at the Academy but neither did she wish to be at home. What she wanted more than anything, she couldn't have and that was to return to a previous life where her mum was still alive. She couldn't explain to people that when her mum had died, her own life had gone on hold. It was like she had forgotten what it was like to be a teen. Everyone else was striving ahead, living their lives with their eyes firmly fixed on the future, ready to further their goals. Their lives were all about enjoying themselves, whilst she felt suspended in an unfamiliar world, not moving further forward, but firmly stuck in a rut she felt unable to climb out of.

Except for Christmas Day, when Stephie had at least made an effort to brighten up their lives and give them some sort of normality, it had been the worst Christmas and New Year holiday Tilly could remember. She certainly didn't want a repeat of it ever again. What had made it even worse, was that on her return to Grantham House, all of the girls had returned full of Christmas and New Year cheer. She was fed up with, 'Hi Tilly. Did you have a good Christmas?' This was Amy. Tilly thought her best friend could have been more understanding.

Then, from Jessica, 'What did you do that was exciting?'

Followed by, 'What presents did you get for Christmas?'

The questions were neverending. No one picked up her mood or the fact that she wasn't answering them. They were all so full of their own lives.

Then, the final straw came from a tall willowy blonde called Isabella, 'Did you go away?'

When Tilly failed to respond enthusiastically, the conversation continued, 'Mum and Dad decided on the spur of the moment to book us all on a flight to Switzerland. I met so many gorgeous guys ... blue eyes and blonde hair! I've made so many new friends and we're all on Snapchat.'

So it went on and on, all about the parties and the gifts. She wished she had a 'Stop' button!

At the end of the first week, Tilly was feeling more despondent than ever and wished that a hole in the ground would open up and swallow her, transporting her to an unknown world where she felt wanted, secure and loved.

After a particularly arduous day, she was just about ready to burst. 'I can't take this anymore. I just can't. I've got to get out of here,' she muttered under her breath. Tilly would admit that she was in a permanent state of living on the edge. She knew that if someone pushed her too far, she'd go over.

After she'd finished her music classes that afternoon she made her way down to the main entrance of Grantham House, signed herself out and began to stride purposely down the long tree-lined drive and through the ornate iron gates that had been there since Franklin House had been a family residence in the early 1800s. She turned right and followed the winding lane which would lead her to the village. Tilly did what she always did when under stress and that was walk. She preferred to walk briskly taking long strides. The repetitive motion of the steps and a breathing technique she'd learned to use before going on stage to perform, which she had found to help her relax, was being used by Tilly on this occasion. In, count to four. Hold the breath for a count of seven. Breathe out slowly for a count of eight. Today it wasn't working.

The village was about a ten-minute walk from the Academy. There wasn't much in the way of shops in the village. The shops in the town held more interest. However, there was a post office that also sold newspapers and magazines, a hairdresser and the cafe which the students referred to as the Coffee

Shop. There was a small supermarket and a pub, which was out of bounds for anyone at the Academy. It wasn't a true village in the English sense of the word. However, it was called that by the locals as it had a great community spirit, local activities and a village type atmosphere and everyone seemed to know everyone else. However, in the last year, it had changed dramatically with the introduction of a monthly craft market on a Saturday which was set up on the main street. Then, on Sunday mornings there was a farmers market where local people could bring in their produce to sell.

The quietness of the country lane, a few horses in the surrounding paddocks and the odd passing car, eased Tilly's mind slightly. However, anyone meeting her could not have failed to notice how tense she was. She planned to visit the local cafe and chill out over a chocolate milkshake. She was hoping that there were no other students who had similar ideas to her. She wanted a complete break from everything to do with the Academy and that included the students.

By the time she arrived, to her dismay, there was only one spare table. She was cross with herself for not remembering that it was market day in the nearby town. But then why would she remember? There was a special bus that left the village around 9 o'clock, returning mid-afternoon. This made it easy for the village retirees to have a weekly trip into the town where there were more shops for them to amble around, more cafes and restaurants for those who wanted to splash out on some of the Special Senior Lunches that were widely advertised. It was also an easy option as they did not have to drive and pay the parking fees which had recently risen.

On this occasion, when they alighted from the bus, it appeared they had all decided to continue the conversations begun on the way home and had all crowded into the village Coffee Shop.

After paying for her order at the cash desk, she managed to push her way past chattering groups of elderly people who had littered the floor with their numerous shopping bags and had found a table tucked away in the back corner of the café. Here she thought she was safe. She felt anti-social, preferring to keep her thoughts to herself and wasn't in the mood for talking. She hadn't been sitting at the table for long when a voice jolted her demanding her attention.

'Hi! It's very busy in here today and I can't see a spare seat. Do you mind if I join you?'

Tilly raised herself from her despondency and looked up with a jolt to find the bluest of eyes looking down straight into hers. In fact, on close inspection, Tilly noticed they were flecked with violet. Tilly was completely thrown off balance and felt her face flushing with embarrassment. What was the matter with her? She, who was always so calm and composed. Before she'd had time to respond, he had woven his way expertly across the tightly packed cafe and had returned from the counter with two milkshakes. 'I thought I'd save the waitress a job, and bring over your order as well.' He continued, 'I haven't seen you around before. I'm Jacques, and your name is?'

Her tummy had done a double flip. She was wondering how she could pick up her drink without her hands shaking. Thankfully, she'd not ordered a latte. At least she didn't have to pick up a milkshake with a straw. She suddenly felt different, an awareness of actually being alive. She felt strange. She hadn't felt like this for a very long time. It seemed as though all of her nerves were on edge and her fingertips were actually tingling. She managed to respond with a tiny voice, 'I'm Tilly.'

It wasn't just the fascination of his eyes. To Tilly, he was the most gorgeous guy she'd ever seen. She had to pinch herself to make sure she wasn't dreaming. He must be a film star or an actor she thought to herself. It was obvious that he worked out. He was toned to perfection. Surely there was no one as handsome as him living in the village! Jessica would have described him as a gorgeous hunk. Thank goodness she's not here, she thought to herself. He had awakened something deep inside her. With his crinkly dark hair and cheeky smile, she was instantly besotted. All her problematic thoughts had suddenly dissolved away.

She couldn't believe it. He was so interested in her. He was asking her questions and certainly didn't appear to find her boring. She had never known anyone who had looked at her like he was doing now, looking at her as though she was the most important person in the world. To Tilly, who had never had a boyfriend, had never had any guy show much interest in her, he was the answer to all her prayers. She felt important. She felt wanted. She opened up to him like a flower that was in bud and was ready to open its petals towards the sun. She told him all about her mum and her dreams of becoming a famous flautist.

The time passed so quickly. Before she knew what had happened, two hours had flown by. Tilly realised on looking at her watch, that they were the only ones left in the coffee shop and the girl behind the counter was staring straight at them with displeasure whilst pointedly tapping at her watch. It was obvious she wanted to close after a full day of standing on her feet. Was there something else, a glimmer of envy? Jacques certainly was a catch.

Suddenly Tilly was jolted into looking at her watch and she immediately panicked. She was due back at the Academy within ten minutes. She wasn't one to break the rules and Jacques noticed she had become distressed.

'Don't worry,' he said, 'my car's parked outside. I'll give you a lift back.'

That was the start of it.

Her mum had always warned, 'Never accept a lift from someone you don't know.'

'Don't worry Mum. I won't,' she'd always replied.

Now sitting beside Jacques in his shiny black Commodore she wondered whether she'd done the right thing. She didn't know him. However, he appeared very caring! He'd even opened the car door for her and had insisted on helping her fasten her seat belt. Wow! At that moment, she felt like royalty. She couldn't believe it. Wait until she told the girls back at the Academy. This kind of thing didn't happen to girls like her. She was the first to admit she wasn't glamorous. She was wearing her Academy jeans and had changed her top, for a plain black shirt, before she had left earlier in the afternoon. The little make-up she'd applied earlier that morning had almost disappeared and, as she had wanted to leave the Academy so quickly, she hadn't even thought about brushing her hair. The ride was short and it got her out of being late – that was all. When Jacques pulled up at the gates, he produced his phone and said, 'Let's have a selfie!'

Before she knew what was happening, he had his arm around her shoulders and she found herself grinning up at the phone. 'I'll send the photo on to you,' and there she was giving him her number and email address. All the advice her mum had given her over the years had been forgotten in an instant.

Chapter 14

When she arrived back on the corridor, she was a different person. The normally reserved Tilly had to stop herself from dancing and singing as she rushed downstairs to the dining room, lighting up the room with a huge grin spread from ear to ear.

Gillie was sitting in the dining room at a table in the corner reserved for the teaching staff. She looked up as Tilly entered. She immediately noticed a radiance she couldn't ever remember seeing in Tilly. Gone were the humped shoulders, the frown, and the dulled expression. She was literally shining from within. Gillie breathed a sigh of relief and said to the member of the teaching staff sitting next to her who just happened to be, Signora De Luca, *the vision*, 'Just look at Tilly. Something good has happened. I wonder what? I haven't seen her look as happy as that for a long time. I've been so worried about her. She's such a private person and I didn't want to intrude.'

'She looks as though she's won a million dollars. She's dancing on air. It must be a guy!' replied *the vision.* 'I'm Italian and I know that look. It's the look of love.'

'You're such a romantic!' the Housemother replied to the Italian teacher.

"The look of love," was the last thing on Gillie's mind. Yes, she wanted Tilly's spirits to rise. She wanted her to be happy but she was unsure about anything else. Tilly hadn't begun to deal with her grief yet. There was a lot for her to work through including her relationship with her father and all of this before her final exams. However, if it was a guy who had brought this sudden transformation, what was the harm? She'd keep an open mind and observe the situation. It would probably fizzle out before it developed. She knew Tilly's main objective was to study overseas. She wasn't stupid. She wouldn't let anything get in the way of that.

When Tilly arrived with her tray at the table she normally shared with Amy and a few others, they looked up in amazement at the smiling Tilly. 'What's happened to you? Where have you been?'

'I've met this gorgeous guy. His name is Jacques and he gave me a ride back from the coffee shop in his car,' replied Tilly as the news bubbled out.

'Lucky you,' said Amy. After Gillie had had the chat with her and she had helped Tilly choose her ball gown, she had decided she hadn't been fair to drop her and join the rest of the girls who were being mean to Tilly behind her back. Their friendship was long-standing, right back to when they had started at the Academy together. Yes, she had become sick of her friend's despondency but she knew Tilly had a good reason to be depressed. However, she was the first to admit, it was rather tiring trying to cheer her up and getting nowhere. She was genuinely pleased for her friend but she would be the first to admit she was also a bit envious. She had longed to have a guy take interest in her but so far, it was a pipe dream. However, something was troubling her. She couldn't put her finger on it. The name, Jacques, sounded familiar but she failed to remember where she'd heard it before.

Tilly was in seventh heaven. She was so entranced by her recent experience, she didn't notice the expressions on the faces of two of the girls, Fiona and Sam, and how they were nudging each other under the table. Gillie, however, was watching the proceedings from across the room with great interest. Both of the senior girls had caused the Housemother great concern in the past. Her mind floated back to a previous incident when both girls had been caught going against Academy rules by climbing out of the windows of their rooms to meet up with some of the guys from the village. These particular guys were notorious for their involvement with drugs and had been in trouble with the police on a previous occasion. On being caught, by one of the Academy security staff on duty that night, a full investigation had been carried out. No drugs had been found. However, it had been necessary to inform the parents of the girls. The girls had been severely reprimanded and warned that if there was a repeat of this type of behaviour, they would find themselves expelled from the Academy. As both of them were high-flyers and planned to take their music studies to a higher level, Gillie had been assured by both of them that they had learnt their lesson and they would never do anything so stupid again. However, Gillie wasn't quite so sure.

Gillie's eyes reverted to Tilly's table. She could see that for the rest of the meal the group was sitting quietly and, in some cases, a few of the girls were mesmerised and couldn't take their eyes away from Tilly. If she had been closer to the table, she would have heard Tilly going on and on about how marvellous Jacques was. Everyone heard about how kind he was, how concerned he was, how gorgeous he was! Gillie transfixed, had noticed that Sam and Fiona were yawning in an exaggerated fashion. They had their phones out, something which was not encouraged at the table. She instantly felt that something was not right. A shiver ran down her spine.

There was such a transformation in Tilly. She couldn't take her eyes away. It was such a contrast to the normal Tilly who, ever since her Mum's death, had sat and picked at her food and couldn't be bothered to show any excitement about anything. Yes, she was more like the old Tilly but there was something else. It was hard to explain. It was as though a light had been switched on and had lit up her whole being. It's said that eyes are the window to a person's soul, well Tilly's eyes were distinctly sparkling. She was animated. She was alive. Gillie could even tell that from across the room. She watched the scene in fascination.

'Is anything wrong?' inquired the Italian *vision*, who had been watching Gillie with interest.

'No, nothing in particular,' she sighed. 'Just thinking what a responsibility I have looking after all of these attractive young women. I always make a point of keeping my ears open and my finger on the pulse, but you never know what may be going off. I can't keep my eyes on them all the time. I suppose girls will be girls and I have to trust that they won't succumb to all those guys in the village who appear to have more money than sense.'

Chapter 15

Tilly was completely unaware that her transformation was causing, not just Gillie, but a whole room full of people to be entranced by her.

Towards the end of the meal, Tilly began to fiddle inside her pocket. Out came her phone, and after checking it, she blushed a vivid shade of pink and said with disbelief, 'He wants to see me again!'

'Wow! When?'

The group was in disbelief. 'He must be keen,' said one.

'What have you got that we haven't?' joked Jessica who always had to be in on the action. Most of the girls appeared impressed, but to Gillie it did not go unnoticed - the mouthing of, 'Shut up,' which was visible on Sam's lips.

Amy did not want to be the one to dampen the spirited Tilly. However, she reminded her, 'Don't forget we aren't allowed to go on dates. You'll have to meet him in the village in the daytime.'

After the meal, everyone returned upstairs to the

common room at the end of the corridor. 'I hope she knows what she's getting into,' voiced Fiona who had hung back from the rest of the group.

'Should we say anything?' asked Sam so quietly so that no one else heard except for her friend.

'Let her have some fun,' replied Fiona. 'She's been so depressed. It'll do her good.'

'What does he see in her?' asked Silvie, who was from Spain and couldn't understand why anyone would be interested in anyone else but her with her dark eyes, long lashes and thick glossy mane of hair, not to mention her model-like figure.

This was followed by, 'We all know what Jacques wants, he gets!' This was followed by uncontrollable giggles from Fiona and Sam.

Amy, by this time, had walked off with Tilly back to their rooms and had not heard this conversation. If she had, she may have voiced her concerns to Tilly. In Tilly's infatuated state, would she have taken any notice?

Back in the common room, the conversation continued. It was the hot topic of the evening. They all agreed that Tilly was attractive but she wasn't hot. 'Not like me!' pouted Sylvie whilst she positioned herself in what she thought was a provocative position. Everyone laughed. Sylvie enjoyed being the centre of attention.

Tilly had said, good night to Amy and had now returned to her room at the end of the corridor. What a day it had been! She was in a state of great euphoria. Her head was up in the clouds, not just ordinary clouds but pure white fluffy ones edged with a silver lining. Delicate pink sequined hearts bobbed alongside in the gentle breeze and the scene would not have been perfect had there not been a flute gently playing a love song. To say she was over the moon didn't come anywhere near to a description of how she felt. She couldn't settle to do anything but walk backward and forwards from one side of her tiny room to the other. She was ecstatic. She was elated.

She suddenly realised that with great relief, the constant weight on her shoulders had lifted. She felt as light as a feather and could imagine herself wafting alongside the clouds and hearts with not a care in the world. For a girl who had been under tremendous stress and grief for so long, it was an uplifting answer to prayer.

It was hard for her to believe that Jacques wanted to see her again! She went over and over reliving the chance meeting, second by second. She analysed each sentence he had said and what she thought he had meant. She kept repeating to herself the whole conversation right from the start, not missing out on anything. He'd even taken a photo! It must mean something.

Tilly had never had a boyfriend. Some of the girls had teased her about her lack of interest in guys. It wasn't that she hadn't been interested. Her life had been on hold. She had been so wrapped up with her Mum and the worry about her illness for so long. That was all she'd had time to cope with along with her music studies at the Academy.

St Celia's was for gifted and talented students, the high achievers who were expected to go out into the world and succeed in their chosen musical field. The Academy was not for time wasters. If you secured a place, you were expected to put all your energies and more into your studies, both in academia and in music.

Tilly was in her final year. She had excelled as a flautist and was all set to continue her studies overseas at one of the top European conservatoires. Her future was planned out like a map. However, this particular evening, her beloved flute remained in its velvet-lined case and her music theory books lay unopened.

Chapter 16

MEANWHILE, BACK IN THE COMMON ROOM, THE conversation surrounding Tilly had developed and had been exaggerated beyond belief. If it had not been for Gillie, who had popped her head around the door and suggested that it was perhaps time for some private study, the conversation would have led to Tilly being engaged and preparing to walk down the aisle.

Gillie had her reasons for her unexpected appearance. It was amazing what you could pick up walking down the corridor, little bits of information that put together would paint a whole picture. However, she needed more clarification, and at that moment, the highly-strung, noisy Jessica's booming voice was giving Gillie some of the answers she required.

It wasn't that Gillie was interfering. It was that her job as a Housemother dictated that she was aware of how her girls were faring mentally, emotionally, physically and educationally. While all of this joviality was going on, Gillie had a sinking feeling in the pit of her stomach. She knew Tilly. The last thing she wanted was the girl being hurt.

In the following weeks, Gillie couldn't help but notice all of the photos that had appeared and were plastered all over Tilly's corkboard on the wall in her room. Some showed her and Jacques together, some were of him on his own, crinkly dark well-groomed hair and tidy beard with his engaging smile.

Gillie couldn't work out what was so special about this guy. It hadn't taken her long to realise that the younger girls were also all besotted with Jacques. He almost had rock star status. Yes, she agreed, he was good looking with a sportsman's physique. He was certainly fit and trim but he wasn't so different from a few others who played cricket on the village green. When she saw one junior girl had scribed his name on her arm in black permanent ink, she knew she had to step in. However, he'd not committed a crime, not that she knew about anyway. She would have to be inventive and think this problem out carefully. She would be the first to admit, she loved her job, but sometimes she wished she was a million miles away. That was how she felt at that moment.

Tilly's peers were causing her a lot of concern. To say they were acting rather strangely was an understatement. Normally, she had a good relationship with all of the girls in Grantham House. They were always ready to share their news with her, photos from home, the latest dress they wanted to purchase and things like that.

At this moment, Gillie didn't really 'get it'. She found small groups of no more than three or four students huddled together whispering in the corridor. Someone always appeared to be on the 'lookout'. There was a definite guiltiness about the way the owner of the phone instantly closed the page when Gillie steered near. The Housemother was concerned. She had a hunch that something wasn't right. This was not normal behaviour. She had tried to find out what was so interesting for the girls to be standing around giggling at shared posts. She'd made light-hearted comments, such as, 'That must be a good joke! Want to share it?'

The focus of their attention appeared to be Instagram. She'd heard references to this so assumed that it was the subject of interest. Gillie wasn't on Instagram but gathered from the threads of conversation that there was a lot of interest in photos. She'd asked Chiara, the Italian teacher, what she knew about the social media platform and she had briefly shown Gillie how it worked.

The latest incident had been when she had heard Jessica's booming voice echoing down the corridor, 'How could she?' and 'I'd die of shame.'

Someone else joined in and said, 'Perhaps we should tell her.'

To which Jessica replied, 'What, and spoil the game!'

This was very perturbing. Gillie knew she wouldn't get very far asking the girls. The best thing Gillie thought would be to inquire from Tilly herself as to what was going on. However, this didn't prove to be so easy. Tilly was in seventh heaven. Whenever Gillie asked her how she was, she appeared to be floating above the clouds. She would give Gillie a beaming smile and reply, 'Couldn't be better, thanks.'

Gillie had noticed that Tilly always seemed to be on her own. Admittedly, she had never been part of the gang of students who grouped in the common room at night and ate toast dripping with butter and jam. However, she'd usually had Amy in tow. It suddenly hit Gillie that she hadn't seen her with Amy recently. Now, she was always rushing off to her room after classes looking very determined and appeared to be focussed on something of great importance.

When Gillie had inquired how Tilly was in class, all her teachers agreed that she had seemed a lot more cheerful and if on some occasions, she appeared to be lacking in concentration, she was still turning out top quality work. Jack Ford, her flute tutor appeared surprised at Gillie's question and responded with, 'Tilly always puts in 100% effort. However, she seems to be far more expressive in her playing than I've ever heard her before.'

Other teachers inquired, 'Why is there a problem? No, everything seems fine.' Gillie began to wonder if she was overreacting.

Perhaps she should ask Amy. However, Amy wasn't forthcoming and shied away from answering any of Gillie's questions. This made matters worse as all she kept replying was, 'I don't know.' The more questions she was asked the more agitated she became. Gillie realising that she was getting nowhere fast, gave up.

What no one knew was how many nights Tilly had been dodging the security men at the main gates at the Academy. Security was tight at St C's. However, Tilly had found a side door leading from the downstairs laundry which had a separate key left on a hook hanging on the inside wall. Tilly couldn't believe her luck. No one bothered to check the laundry at night.

With everyone chattering away in the common room, she was able to slip downstairs, unlock the door from the inside, lock the door from the outside and follow an unused track through the bush which was now largely overgrown. It had been originally used for emergency vehicles in the case of a bush fire but it was still accessible by someone on foot and with the torchlight shining from her phone, she could see quite well. This track led onto the lane well hidden by trees and undergrowth. By climbing over a wooden fence Tilly was able to join Jacques who had been sitting waiting in his car. And so the pattern had been set.

Tilly wasn't stupid. She had to cover her tracks. One thing that she always did when leaving her room to meet up with Jacques, was to take her flute case with her. If anyone saw her, she could always tell them she was on her way to the Music Block. On a few occasions, she had seen Gillie in the distance and had quickly turned around to head in the direction of the Block. No-one stopped her to ask any questions. When she knew she was safe, she would alter her direction and return to the bush track. So far she had not been caught out.

Under normal circumstances, Tilly wasn't a girl who broke the rules. However, Tilly had not been living in normal circumstances for a long while. Her mum's long complicated illness had been hard to take. She had felt that no one understood what she had been going through. Jacques was the answer to her prayers. He had been the one to show her tenderness and compassion. He had listened to her. He had been the one to shower her with the attention she so desperately needed. Tilly had never experienced anything like this before. He was the one who had wrapped her tightly in his arms while she had cried and he was the one who had kissed away her tears. He had made her feel complete. He had made her feel that life was worth living again.

Chapter 17

At the same time as Tilly had met Jacques, she had also acquired a split personality. One half showed that she was still keeping up with her studies. She had always lived for her private flute lessons with Mr Ford and had, so far, not allowed anything to stand in their way. However, the other half of her was now living in a glorious shiny bubble where she was ensconced with Jacques and no one else had access to enter. She couldn't wait for classes to end. Phones were banned during class times but, like everyone else, as soon as classes finished she couldn't wait to get to her room fast enough to check her texts.

Official dates with a guy were banned at the Academy unless it was a very special occasion endorsed by a parent. The Academy was very strict as it had full responsibility for the students.

Amy had sensed that something wasn't right with her best friend. Something suspicious had been going on for a while now but she wasn't sure what was happening. Tilly had become vague and had become an expert in not answering questions directed to her. All she would tell Amy was that, 'Everything's fine. It couldn't be better. No need to worry.'

This change in Tilly was a concern. She'd altered but not for the best. Amy realised she hardly ever saw Tilly in the evenings. After the study period had finished, the majority of the girls would meet up to catch up on the day in the common room, listen to music or watch a movie borrowed from the library. It was strange that no one seemed to realise that Tilly was missing. If they did realise, then they didn't say anything. She had become so obsessed with Jacques that she had, in the opinion of some of the girls, become 'a bore'. Jessica stated, 'I'm sick of hearing about him.'

Amy had knocked on Tilly's door a few times just before going back to her room to go to bed and had received no reply. This had set her mind racing. When was the last time she'd knocked on the door and Tilly had answered? She racked her brain. OMG! She suddenly realised that it had been weeks, not days. When Gillie had stopped her in the corridor and had invited her into her flat for a hot chocolate, she had guessed what it was all about. She had tried to refuse the invitation but the forceful expression on Gillie's face told her it wasn't an invitation she could refuse.

'How are you?' she began as she busied herself in the kitchen of the small flat. Before she'd had time to answer, it was followed by, 'I haven't seen you and Tilly around together for a while. Is everything OK?'

Amy admired Gillie. She didn't want to tell tales so she sat on the settee twisting the mug of hot chocolate around in her hands. This didn't go unnoticed by Gillie. 'You're going to burn your hands. Put the mug down and tell me what's troubling you.'

Amy felt very uncomfortable. Tilly had been a good friend ever since the two girls had begun their studies at the Academy. They had been very supportive of each other and the last thing she wanted was to get Tilly into trouble. She folded her arms around her as if giving herself a comforting hug and stared into space hoping the right words would come into her head.

'It's Tilly, isn't it?' Gillie asked tentatively.

Amy thought the less she said would be better. She fixed her eyes on the view she could see through the window and said, 'I hardly see her now. She always seems to be too busy to spend time with me. I really don't know what's going on.'

In all truthfulness, Amy didn't know what was going on but she had a good idea. Jessica and her girlfriends, mainly Sam and Fiona, were reported to be making comments such as, 'Do you think they've done it yet?'

Students witnessed the pair doubled up in uncontrollable fits of giggling. When this filtered back to Amy, she felt sick to the stomach.

'Do you think he'll announce it on Instagram?' Fiona had been reported asking with a hint of sarcasm.

Sam had replied, 'Oh, you're just jealous.'

At that moment, Signora De Luca had appeared and had reprimanded them in rapid Italian for being late for her Italian class. She had found the girls' behaviour had been uncontrollable during the lesson and their continuous giggling and whispering had forced her to report them to the administration. Fortunately, for Sam and Fiona, she had not heard the comments that had led them to become so out of control.

Amy was sure that Tilly was completely unaware of all the attention she was receiving as a result of her relationship with Jacques. If she had been aware, Amy knew that she would have been horrified if she'd realised the rumours that were floating around every corner of the Academy were at her expense. What was Tilly getting into? Amy certainly didn't want to know.

Gillie, however, felt that Amy's guarded reactions to her questions had reinforced her theory that Tilly's secretive behaviour was hiding something. She knew she had to investigate further.

Chapter 18

THERE WERE NO WORDS TO DESCRIBE HOW DAN FELT. If it hadn't been for Stephie, he didn't know how he would have coped. After Christmas, he had continued his visits to her house.

His dad continued on the theme that Stephie wasn't needed. 'I don't know why you want to keep going round there,' he would say to Dan. His son usually ignored him. It just wasn't worth making the effort to respond. However, Stephie had been a lifeline to Dan. He had called round to her place as often as he could. He found relief in talking to her about his mum and the best times were when he accompanied her on her walks with Dizzy around the park.

Stephie adored dogs. On her walks with Dan and Dizzy, she often shared her doggie stories with him. She had been a volunteer at the local dogs' refuge for a while now.

'Did I tell you about Scruffy?' she asked on one of their walks.

'No, I don't think so,' replied Dan wondering what was so special about this dog and the reason for the choice of name. There was always something unusual about the dogs that were left at the refuge. Some of the stories Stephie shared with him were amusing and some were terribly sad. She also loved to go into great detail when describing the people who came to visit the refuge to choose a new dog.

'Oh, it's so sad,' she said. 'He was found cowering by the side of the road. A young couple with a small child found him and brought him in. They wondered if he'd been run over. They'd had to pick him up as he didn't appear able to walk. He was referred to the local vet who said that, after he'd been X-rayed, he had a broken leg. On closer examination, he also showed evidence of being beaten. The dog was so frightened, even the vet, who was used to animals, found it difficult to comfort the dog and secretly had thought putting the dog to sleep would have been the best option. However, there was something about this dog. He seemed to have lost the will to live. Perhaps he deserved a second chance? With the help of the vet nurse, Scruffy was given an anaesthetic and his broken leg was covered in a cast. He was then taken back to the refuge where one of the volunteers took him home to look after him until he was well enough to return. He'd been at the refuge ever since. 'He's a sweet looking little dog, a rough-haired terrier but no one seems to want him,' volunteered Stephie.

'Why not? What's wrong with him?' asked Dan.

'There's nothing physically wrong with him now. His leg is OK and his wounds from the beatings have healed but I think he's depressed and scared. When dogs are brought in from the street, you never know where they've come from and what their history is. When people come to visit the refuge to look for a dog, they want either a puppy or a cheerful, waggly tail sort of dog. Scruffy must have been badly ill-treated. He seems afraid of people and just cowers in his bed in a corner of his kennel.'

'Can I visit the refuge with you next time you go?'

Unbeknown to Dan, Stephie had been waiting for the right moment to suggest that Dan accompany her to the refuge. She was delighted with his interest in Scruffy and his enthusiasm for accompanying her. She had carried this idea around in her head ever since she'd first introduced Dan to the dog park.

'Of course, you can. I'm on the roster for this Saturday afternoon. If you want to come you're more than welcome. Just ask your dad if it's OK and I'll give you a lift there and back.'

Dan thought bitterly that his dad really couldn't care less where he was on a Saturday afternoon.

It was the first time since his mum had died that he'd been able to take an interest in anything outside of his normal routine. The more he thought of Scruffy, the more he realised that he couldn't wait for Saturday to arrive. He had to admit to himself that he was quite excited about the visit to the refuge. He wished he could share the news with his sister but her phone always seemed to be off and she had stopped replying to the emails and texts he'd sent her. He was sure that something was wrong. It wasn't like Tilly to cut herself off like this. He'd mentioned it to his dad but he seemed unconcerned and offered in his now usual uninterested monotone, 'I expect she's busy.'

Dan thought he'd mention it to Stephie. Perhaps she could shed some light on it.

Eventually, Saturday arrived and Dan counted the hours until 2 o'clock. He'd suggested it may be better if he walked to Stephie's home and they could go together to the dogs' refuge in Stephie's car. He'd mentioned it to his dad but as he was dozing in the armchair, it hadn't created much of a response.

It was going to be a relief to go to visit the dogs. It would take his mind off all his other problems even if it was only for an hour or so. Pete had now transferred a lot of his business to a home office and had thankfully decided to employ a cook/cleaner, a Mrs Greene who had recently retired but needed to earn some extra money. She came in three days a week. At least the house was cleaner and tidier and they were guaranteed a decent meal. However, in some ways, his dad working from home had made the situation worse. He seemed to have given up on the world and apart from his work and speaking to his clients, he rarely left the house.

Stephie said, 'You seem very quiet this afternoon. Is everything OK?'

'I suppose so. I'm really looking forward to visiting the dogs but I was wondering if you'd heard from Tilly. She used to ring home every Sunday evening without fail. I can't understand why she's not phoning. I've rung her at least once a week. When I texted her she says she's too busy to chat on a Sunday evening. I don't get it. She was never too busy when Mum was here.'

'Come to think of it, I've not heard from her recently either,' replied Stephie. 'I'll try to ring her this evening, OK? Don't worry; your dad is probably right. I'll let you know when I hear from her.'

Stephie didn't want to alarm Dan but the more she thought about it, the more she realised she hadn't heard much from Tilly either. After the Christmas long break, Tilly had begun texting her on a fairly regular basis but now she thought about it, she realized that the number of texts had died down. She hoped there was nothing wrong. It wasn't like Tilly to not reply to messages. She left Dan alone with his thoughts so she could concentrate on the traffic as she drove down the winding road.

Dan thought's drifted back to when his mum had been alive and his sister had practically phoned every day, sometimes more than once, to chat with his mum. All the news had tumbled out. They had discussed everything and his dad had joked about it, 'I can't get a word in edgeways. I don't know how women can keep talking for so long. I just don't get it.'

His wife had laughed and replied, 'Oh, so you never talk? What about when you go to the pub for a quick drink and return two hours later and the dinner's cold and ruined!'

Dan desperately needed to talk to Tilly and for Tilly to respond to him, to show him she cared. He was getting no conversation from Pete who was in the depths of depression and could hardly utter a word when he wasn't working.

What was the matter with his sister? The last time he had managed to speak to her, she had been evasive, had said everything was great and she was really busy. When he'd questioned her she'd given him one-word answers and told him she was too tired to talk. What was that all about?

At least Stephie always had time for him.

'Here we are,' she said, hoping the visit to the dogs' refuge would divert Dan's mind away from his sister and all his other problems. As Stephie drove into the uneven gravel car park, a jolly-looking, but a rather untidy lady waved from behind the wire gates. Stephie waved back and they both got out of the car and walked towards her. Cheerfully, she said, 'Hi Stephie! How are you?' Before Stephie had had time to respond, she'd continued, 'You must be Dan. How are you? I'm Claudia.'

Dan thought that her appearance certainly didn't fit in with being a Claudia. He imagined someone with a name like Claudia would be a glamorous movie star. This lady was dressed in army camouflage with her trousers stuffed into waterproof boots. She was well-proportioned and had a leather belt wrapped around her middle and resembled a parcel tied up with string. Her hair was a sort of ginger and she had a knitted bobble hat in bright yellow perched on the back of her head. This didn't cover all of her hair and strands were sticking out at various angles. She certainly would stand out in a crowd. However, she seemed friendly enough and if she cared for dogs her heart must be in the right place.

She was the complete opposite to Stephie, who apart from her sometimes unruly blonde curls, was always dressed neatly and tidily. She took pride in her appearance and Dan had never seen her without wearing any make-up. Today, she was dressed in smart casual. Her jeans, windcheater, and sneakers would have been adequate for going into town. However, she'd come prepared for dirty work by bringing her rubber gloves and bright red wellies!

'How's Scruffy?' Stephie asked.

'Just the same. The leg has healed well but he's not a happy fella. He must have been ill-treated as he doesn't seem to trust people. When people go near him, he cowers in the corner and shakes. It's so upsetting.'

'Can I see him?' asked Dan tentatively.

'Of course you can. Follow me but don't expect instant results. He's not like Dizzy. Don't expect licks and a waggly bottom.'

Dizzy never just wagged her tail - her whole bottom swayed from side to side as she swished her tail in wide swipes. She always greeted Dan with such enthusiasm. It was hard for him to imagine a dog who was so frightened of people.

Dan asked a question which he'd had on his mind ever since he'd heard about the dog. 'Why is he called Scruffy?'

Stephie explained to him that when the dog had been brought in, he had looked so dirty with matted hair. Immediately Claudia had looked at him and had commented in her no-nonsense fashion, 'My! He's a scruffy looking animal!' So the name Scruffy had remained.

Stephie and Dan were led through two sets of locked wire gates and along a corridor of cages. Claudia continued to the end of the corridor and pointed to the last cage on the right. 'He's in here,' she said pointing to her right. 'We keep him away from the other dogs at the moment. He seems too afraid to play with them.'

She unlocked the cage door and Dan peered into the dark dingy enclosure. Right at the back, in the corner huddled on a canvas dog bed that looked as though it had seen better days, was a bundle of salt and peppered grey fur, slightly matted and standing out were two black ears that were pointing away from his face and laid flat against his head. He turned slightly away from his visitors and began to quiver.

Dan peered at the dog and felt so much pity. It was as though a tap had been turned on and he felt he wanted to cry. However, he bit his lip and tried to hide his emotions. Here was a dog who knew what it was like to feel lonely and afraid. He felt an instant comradeship with the dog. He recognised something in the dog, a need to be loved, a need to be wanted.

'Can I go and sit with him?'

'Of course you can,' whispered Claudia, 'but don't expect much of a response.'

Dan entered the cage slowly. He bent down, as to appear smaller, so as not to threaten the dog and crouched down in the opposite corner. Stephie realised what he was doing and tugged on Claudia's sleeve. The two women nodded at each other as if in a conspiracy. Together they quietly left Dan to work a miracle.

Dan didn't attempt to speak to the dog. He didn't move closer to the dog and he certainly didn't try to touch him. Something was happening inside him. He didn't know what it was but he felt so much compassion for this scrap of fur.

After about ten minutes, the dog began to take notice of Dan. He shuffled around to face him but still hadn't the confidence to look directly at Dan. Dan was sure that the shaking wasn't so evident. He didn't want to spoil the situation by startling the dog. However, he shuffled ever so slightly out of his corner on the cold concrete floor and moved slightly towards

Scruffy. The dog watched him and even pricked up his ears. That was an improvement thought Dan to himself. Some sixth sense told him to go no further that day but he'd decided he'd be back.

When Stephie returned to the cage, she saw that Dan had moved closer to the dog and that in response, the awful shivering and shaking had stopped. She whispered, 'Time for home Dan.'

He turned slowly away from the dog and keeping his body low to the ground as he had done when he had entered the cage, he crawled his way in silence to the door, raised himself as slowly from the concrete as he was able and walked back along the corridor into the sunshine.

'I'd like to come again,' he replied to Claudia's question of how things had gone. She nodded her response and unbeknown to him, she gave a thumbs-up sign to Stephie. 'Well that seemed to go alright,' said Stephie. 'I think he liked you.'

Dan hardly spoke a word on the ride home. This didn't go unnoticed by Stephie. She realised that the dog and Dan had a lot in common and that perhaps something was happening between them. She raised a silent prayer of thanks. She had always believed that people, or in this case dogs, were sent into your life for a purpose. You just had to wait for the magic to happen.

'Please can I go again?' Before Stephie had time to answer, he continued, 'When are you next on the roster?'

'Well, I'm not rostered to go for another week but I could drop you off tomorrow afternoon if you like. There are some things I need to discuss with Claudia about the Fete they're holding to raise funds. How do you feel about that?'

Dan beamed his response. His expression said it all. 'Come down tomorrow at about 2 o'clock but don't forget to run it by your dad.'

'Oh, he won't mind,' muttered Dan as he left.

'I'll give Tilly a call this evening,' she shouted as an afterthought. She certainly needed to know what was going on. She remembered her promise to Jo that she would keep an eye on both Dan and Tilly.

Chapter 19

It was now May. Tilly had been floundering for a while. The sickness had been making her physically weak. The continual worry was causing her to lose more weight. It had been so hard keeping up with everything. She had had so much on her mind. It was getting out of hand.

Then there were the arguments that Jacques had been provoking. She couldn't believe how he'd changed. He demanded that he see her every night and that wasn't possible. She had tried to reason with him and explain to him that she had been feeling so ill and tired and that she had found it difficult to cope with her academic work. He couldn't see the point in all her studying. He had not been able to accept that she was adamant about fulfilling her lifelong dream of travelling to either London or Paris.

'What do you want to go there for? All this studying is a waste of time. You'll never be famous. You need to get out there and find a job and earn some money,' was his usual way of remonstrating with her.

More than once he had threatened that he would finish their relationship and kept boasting that he had a long list of girls just waiting to fill her shoes.

Tilly was aware that her relationship with Jacques was being followed closely by some of the senior students, especially Jessica, Fiona, and Sam. It was even rumoured that some of the younger students had begun to follow him on Social Media. She heard them talking about him and how they wanted to be his friend on Snapchat. She knew that there were one or two girls who desperately wished they were in her shoes. There had been snide comments. Fiona had suggested, 'Tell your Jacques, that when he's finished with you, I'll be waiting for him.' She'd then run off in a fit of giggles to report to her friend Sam. Presently, Tilly wished she'd never set eyes on Jacques.

Ever since the sickness began, Tilly had been beside herself with worry. Now she was petrified. When questioned, she'd insisted she had a gastric bug that was making her so ill. She felt completely isolated. She had never been part of the crowd. Her circumstances had dictated that she couldn't give herself freely to let herself go and act like any other seventeen-year-old. Since her return to the Academy, after her Mum's death, she had developed into a loner and her friendship with Amy had deteriorated. It was not intentional. It was purely due to what Tilly described as everyone else's inability to understand her and her needs.

She thought back to when she had first met Jacques. He had appeared to have understood her. Well, she thought, he had at the time. He was the one who had said, 'Ignore them all Tilly. I'm here for you. I'll take care of you.'

How things can change! At first, he had been the answer to her prayers. She could tell him everything. However, lately, things had been turning sour. She couldn't pinpoint the exact moment when this had begun to happen. Was it before she'd begun to be ill? Perhaps it was when she told him about the sickness?

It was now she desperately needed a friend. She had wracked her brains thinking of someone who would listen to her without criticism. She just couldn't talk to her father about the things that were taking over her mind. She knew what his reaction would be. Oh no! That would be too terrifying a prospect! Her brother wasn't able to help. He was too young. What about Stephie? She had considered phoning Stephie but she couldn't. She knew that if she confided her fears to Stephie, that although she'd try to help, she would be so disappointed in her. No, she couldn't go that way.

Tilly was in a fix. She didn't know how to deal with it. Jacques was no longer interested in her. If she confided her fears to Gillie, in her role as Housemother, she would have to inform her dad. Cynthia, Jacques' Mum, had always been very kind to her, but no, it wasn't possible to speak to her either. What was bothering Tilly wasn't a subject that she felt able to talk about to anyone. She felt so ashamed and riddled with guilt.

Never before had she so longed to experience the tummy gripes she normally suffered from each month. She'd spent hours on Google researching her symptoms. She had read that high levels of stress could cause periods to stop. That fitted. Now, she was weighing up in her mind whether she was stressed, due to the nausea and lack of periods, or was she just suffering from stress and that was causing her problems. She was so emotional and kept bursting into tears for no reason at all. Now she'd noticed that everyone seemed to be avoiding her and staring at her from afar.

'What's the matter with you?' Amy had asked her only a few nights earlier. 'I know you're feeling ill with this bug but do you have to be so snappy? I wish you'd never met Jacques. You were never as bad-tempered as this before you met him. I wish you'd go to the doctor and get yourself sorted. Do you know people are talking about you? They just daren't say anything to you because whatever they say is wrong. I'm beginning to feel the same way!' and out of the room, she stormed. Tilly burst into tears again.

The next time Amy saw her walking along the corridor, she was shocked beyond belief at the change in Tilly's appearance. She was so thin and her huge hazel eyes seem to be standing out so prominently in contrast to the paleness of her complexion. She had bravely confronted her saying, 'Tilly, you can't go on like this. You look awful! I'm really worried about you. Why don't you go to the doctor? He'll be able to give you something to make you feel better.'

Following Tilly's lead, she continued, 'A stomach bug shouldn't still be bothering you.'

Tilly found it hard to believe Amy was so naive that she believed Tilly was suffering from was a gastric upset. Her response was immediate. She turned away from Amy so there was no eye contact, drew herself up to full height and said abruptly, 'I'll go next week if I don't feel any better. I'm sure I'll be OK soon. It's just a nasty tummy bug. Stop fussing.'

On saying these words, Tilly walked off in the direction of her room leaving a perplexed Amy standing in the corridor with a very worried expression on her face.

'What has she done? I do hope it's not what I think it is,' she said to herself.

Chapter 20

What was even worse than the outburst with Amy was the incident on the lane a few nights later. That was ten times worse. Tilly was reeling from the shock. The argument had been witnessed from afar by a group of girls on their way home from the coffee shop. She prayed they were too far away to hear what was being said. She desperately hoped they were.

Tilly kept going over and over what Jacques had said or rather shouted, 'What do you mean, you're scared you may be pregnant?'

At his response, she had cringed in fear like an animal caught in the headlights of a car. She was unable to move and feeling faint had clung onto the door handle in desperation. This was not how it was meant to be. Jacques' eyes appeared black as coals and anger emanated from every part of his body. His utter disgust and loathing were written across his face. With greater urgency, he had demanded, banging his fist on the roof of his car, 'Well, have you done a pregnancy test?'

When she didn't respond he continued, 'You haven't, have you? How did I get mixed up with an innocent like you? Anyway, how do I know it's not someone else's brat? Well, don't expect me to support you. Don't blame me.'

With that, he had jumped in his car, slammed the door and sped off at top speed leaving her standing shell-shocked in the lane. She felt demoralised and sullied. She felt used. She felt like crawling into a hole where she could hide, later to reappear into a world where none of this trauma had happened.

How Tilly managed to stagger back to her room, she didn't know. She couldn't just walk in the front door and through the entrance hall. There were always people there walking to and from their rooms. People would want to know what the matter was. She couldn't hide the fact she was so upset. Her mascara running down her cheeks and the constant shaking was a giveaway. She made her way round to the laundry door and hoped it would be unlocked. For once, luck was on her side.

It was obvious that Jacques no longer wanted to see her. The mere hint of a possible pregnancy had seen him running in the opposite direction as fast as he was able. He had made it quite plain that he wanted nothing more to do with her and blamed her for the pregnancy. He had told her, 'You were the one who came onto me. Don't blame me. You got what you wanted.'

Tilly had been horrified at his words. The charming guy who had been so kind and understanding, and who had treated her like a delicate Princess, had changed overnight into a raging animal.

After the argument on the lane, Tilly was jolted into the realisation that Jacques wasn't the guy she thought he'd been. Had he been stringing her along ever since she met him with just one thought in his head? Had she been part of an elaborate game where the prize had been for her to lose her virginity? She shuddered at the thought. She was just as bad as a whole lot of other girls, taken in by a good looking guy who'd taken her for a ride.

She was horrified. She wouldn't even be surprised if his mates had put bets down as to how soon he could sleep with her.

On arrival back in her room, she hurriedly retrieved her phone from her bag as it was signalling a text had arrived. It couldn't have been blunter. The message said, 'Dumped! LOL!'

Hurt – yes! Humiliated – yes! Was she surprised? No, deep down in the depths of her heart, she wasn't. Dumped by a Smartphone message! No explanation. Nothing! How could he? How could he?

Tilly was beside herself. With rage pulsating through her body and an energy surge that came as a result of the anger she felt, she unleashed her fury in the only way she could think of at that moment. She rushed to the corkboard and attacked it with vigour, pulling off the photos of her and Jacques taken in happier times. She viciously ripped each one up into tiny pieces and one by one dumped them into the bin. At the same time, she unleashed a tirade of expletives aimed at the absent Jacques. Words that were not in Tilly's normal vocabulary were hurled into the air. Did it make her feel any better? It may have reduced her pent up emotion but no, nothing could make her feel better at that moment.

How did she feel afterwards? If anything, she felt worse. The situation hadn't altered. She was still in the same position. When there were no more words, she collapsed onto her bed, curling herself into a ball. It didn't take long for her whole body to be racked by shuddering sobs.

Amy had heard about the altercation in the lane. You couldn't help hearing about it. It was the hot topic of conversation that evening. Although Amy had not been so close to Tilly since she had been seeing Jacques, she was still concerned about her. She heard the sobs as she stood outside her friend's door. Things must be really bad she thought. With a quiet knock on the door, and not waiting for an answer, she tentatively turned the knob and opened the door.

The normally composed Tilly was by now sitting scrunched up on her bed, rocking backward and forwards, head held tightly over her knees. Amy realised that things were worse than she'd anticipated. Positioning herself next to her friend on the bed, wrapping her arms around her and hugging her tightly until the rocking had stopped and the sobs had quietened down.

'Oh, Tilly! Is it what I think it is?'

Tilly responded with a nod and again burst into heavy, heart-wrenching sobs.

Amy continued to hold on tightly and wait until Tilly was composed enough to talk.

'What are you going to do?' whispered Amy recognising that Tilly was beyond herself and needed a soft approach.

Tilly, white-faced, muttered under her breath, 'What can I do?'

'Have you done a pregnancy test?' she whispered.

'No,' Tilly replied shaking of her head.

'Don't you think it would be a good idea – just to make certain?' asked Amy.

'I don't think that would change the circumstances.'

'No, but it would tell you how many weeks which would give you an idea what your options are.'

Inside, Tilly was a jumbled mess. She now had to admit to herself what she already knew and had known for a few weeks now. She did not need to visit the doctor to find out what was wrong with her. The lapse in her monthly periods, the morning sickness and the tightness of her pants, especially around her waist, were all the symptoms she needed. You didn't need to visit a doctor to be told you were pregnant.

'If you are pregnant, have you thought about what you're going to do? Are you going to keep the baby or are, you know, planning on having an abortion?' Amy asked tentatively.

Tilly ran her fingers through her hair in desperation. By now she had risen from the bed and was pacing the floor in anguish. 'No,' she uttered, shaking her head from side to side, 'I don't think so. I know abortion is probably the most sensible thing to do, but I can't explain my decision. I've spent hours on the internet looking at sites to do with everything on pregnancy. I've visited Family Planning Australia and Pregnancy Health so many times; I know the information off by heart. Whatever site you suggest, I've visited it. You name it and I've been there.'

Having stopped the pacing, she turned to face Amy with such anguish written across her face. 'I feel sick with the confusion and I'm so scared. It's not just about me, is it? Mum was always against abortion and she always used to say, she couldn't understand how anyone could go ahead with it. I don't want to have a baby. I wish it would all go away but I can't kill it and that's what I'd be doing. I couldn't live with myself if I went ahead with it. Years later I'd be wondering what my baby would have been like as it grew up. Someone, please help me,' she begged.

Amy felt like a caged animal. She was completely out of her depth. By now, she had moved away from Tilly and was standing next to the door. She had a desperate urge to escape. The emotional energy in the room hung heavy in the air like a thick fog. Of course, she was sorry for her friend but a part of her blamed Tilly for the situation she had got herself into. However, Amy wasn't an unfeeling girl and with arms outstretched, she walked the few steps across to Tilly and gently hugged her. Quietly, she whispered, 'I don't know how to help. You'll have to tell someone.'

By now, Tilly was becoming very agitated. She was gulping back the tears and was wringing her hands together. 'I can't tell anyone. My Dad will kill me. He'll be so angry and ashamed. I've ruined everything. Everything I've always wanted is disappearing like water down a drain. Please don't tell anyone Amy,' she implored as she looked at her friend in desperation.

Amy turned and walked the few steps towards the door shaking her head and trying to not show that she was also on the verge of tears. She, like Tilly, was only seventeen. She'd never experienced such a situation as this. It was too hard to handle. 'You'll have to do something soon otherwise everyone will know. Think about it,' she said without looking at her friend.

As she left the room, she felt drained. She knew she had to do something. As she walked back along the corridor to her room, she thought of all the things she should have said to Tilly but knew it was too late and certainly wouldn't have helped the situation. The conversation in her head went along these lines,

'I don't know how you could have got yourself in such a fix. Didn't you know he was the village stud? You should have had more sense. He's always been after only one thing. We thought you knew!'

She imagined Tilly responding with, 'Why didn't you warn me?'

'Because you were so obsessed with him, you wouldn't have taken any notice.'

'But he was always so kind and understanding and that's what I liked about him. I could talk to him.'

Amy shook her head in disbelief.

Chapter 21

AFTER TILLY'S MASSIVE MELTDOWN, SHE WAS LEFT ON her own for the remainder of the evening. Thankfully, the sickness had finally stopped. According to the websites she had looked at, it could mean she was around 10 weeks pregnant. A cold sweat ran through her tense body.

Tilly didn't know what to do. Thoughts of desperation were raging inside her head. She couldn't think straight. Amy had suggested abortion. She knew she'd shunned it, but could it be an option? How would she arrange something like that on her own? She certainly didn't want anyone knowing anything about it. It was all too difficult.

Above all, was the shame. She thought about her mum. What would she have thought? 'If Mum had still been alive, I wouldn't be in this position,' she said aloud to no one in particular. Dad will kill me. Her mind was a whirl of incoherent thoughts. She wasn't emotionally stable enough to be making any decisions at the moment. Perhaps if she slept, in the morning it would all appear like a bad dream.

When she had first started meeting Jacques, he had been so charming and apart from the goodnight hug and a kiss, he'd not tried to go any further. Tilly had trusted him. He had been so caring and concerned. The thoughts of needing contraception had never entered her mind. 'How stupid can you get?' she muttered to herself.

There'd only been one occasion when things had gone further. Tilly hadn't expected anything to happen. She wasn't naive. However, this particular evening, she'd been particularly upset and was missing her mum terribly. It started just as a friendly hug but it wasn't long before things got out of hand. It had happened so quickly.

Tilly couldn't blame Jacques as she felt she'd been a willing partner. Just once wouldn't matter, would it? She remembered mum had told her that she had waited a long time before she'd become pregnant. Foolishly, she reassured herself, I'll be fine. Nothing will happen.

However, after the event, she'd had time to think it over. She'd made the decision it wasn't going to happen again. Jacques had become more and more demanding. He reasoned, 'Why stop when you've done it once ... and you enjoyed it!' he'd sneered. She didn't want to take a chance again. Even going on the pill wasn't the answer for her; she didn't want anything to stand in the way of her career. That was what was most important to her and she wasn't going to take any chances. None at all.

Chapter 22

Cynthia was emptying the dishwasher. Mugs and glasses in the cupboard above the counter, plates in the cupboard underneath, cutlery in the top drawer under the breakfast bar. It wasn't a difficult job. It was a task she did daily. She could almost do it blindfolded. This morning, however, it was taking ages. This morning, her mind was on other things.

Jacques' outburst after breakfast, before he had left for work, had got to her.

'I don't know how she is! I don't care how she is! Anyway, it's none of your business!' He'd stormed out the door, revved up his car and left in a cloud of red dust.

He wasn't normally like that when she inquired about Tilly. She'd only asked, 'How's Tilly? She hasn't called around lately.'

The more she thought about it, the more concerned she became. In her mind, she went over the previous week. It was only now she realised that Jacques hadn't been his normal chirpy, cheeky self. She recounted the times he'd been abrupt and recalled him earlier in the week, shouting, 'I'm going out and don't ask me where. I'll be home when I'm home.'

At times, he could be moody but these episodes didn't usually last long. He'd spend some time alone in his room accompanied by blaring music or he'd go for a jog and return fine. When she'd mentioned to Derek, her husband, 'Jacques seems to be a bit down in the dumps.'

Derek had replied, 'Stop fussing and leave him alone. He's probably had a tiff with Tilly. He'll be back to normal, you'll see.'

That was exactly what Cynthia was hoping for. She couldn't settle until he was back to his charming self.

From being a teenager, all Cynthia had wished and longed for was to get married and have a large family. She felt that was her destiny, a large brood of children and then grandchildren. She was a born mother, perhaps a bit too clucky at times. However, there was an empty feeling deep down inside her. It didn't matter what she did, it was always there. That's probably why she had chosen to work in child care. Holding a child in her arms made her feel complete.

After her marriage to Derek, she easily became pregnant with her first baby, but unfortunately lost the daughter she had hoped for. This was the pattern to follow, two more lost babies, one a boy and then another girl. Then, with the specialist's help, and IVF treatment, she had managed to become pregnant and gave birth to a healthy, bouncing boy, her beautiful, perfect Jacques!

At first, she couldn't believe it. She would sit for ages just staring at his deep blue eyes with their violet flecks, his dark curly eyes lashes which any girl would have died for. Then there was his smile, no one else ever smiled for her like Jacques. From the moment of his birth, she was obsessed with him and he could do no wrong. Jacques not only received all the love a mother could give, but he also received all the bottled up emotions that had been stored away for the lost babies. To say he was adored and worshipped was no understatement. Derek sometimes felt completely abandoned. Cynthia was besotted with her son.

It was only now that his mother was starting to realise and admit to herself, that her only son was turning out to be a totally spoilt, and sometimes a very selfish young man, who was not always considerate of the feelings of others. He had no idea how his recent comments had upset her.

Although Jacques was only nineteen, he was in some ways very immature for his age. Cynthia thought back over the number of times he'd come to her to sort out his problems. She had been only too willing, to make phone calls on his behalf with excuses to girls he didn't want to see or had lost interest in because he had found another girl who was more attractive than the last one.

'He'll never grow up if you keep stepping in,' Derek told his wife firmly. 'He'll never be responsible for his actions ... and something else, stop giving him money. He's earning a good wage. Let him pay his bills.'

Cynthia's thoughts had been dwelling on Jacques' behaviour over the past week or so. She knew her son. Knew he had faults. Knew that she was to blame for some of them. However, she would never admit it, especially to her husband.

Jacques could be extremely charming and polite when he wanted to be. He was exceptionally good looking and with all the manual work he did on the cars, followed by his fitness regime at the gym, he wasn't lacking in girls waiting to catch his eye.

Cynthia had been very surprised by his latest choice, Tilly. She wasn't the normal type of girl her son chose. She wasn't flashy and a follower of the latest fashion trends. She certainly didn't have the tattoos and bright pink hair that the previous girlfriend had felt was so important. Tilly was completely different, so very different, that it had been a cause for concern.

She had only just turned seventeen. Cynthia knew she was a final year student and boarder at St Celia's Academy of Music. Cynthia didn't need to be told that Tilly was a gifted and talented musician. She knew the Academy only took the best. In this case, Tilly was a flautist with a promising future.

Cynthia was the first to admit that Tilly was a bit of a puzzle. She was quite delightful, well mannered and spoke with a refined accent. However, she wasn't snooty and stuck-up like some of the Academy girls who gave the impression they thought themselves superior to everyone else in the village. Cynthia didn't know why her son was so attracted to the girl. They seemed to have little in common.

Tilly had visited the house only a few times. On these occasions, she had mentioned how excited she was about graduating from the Academy and taking up a place at one of the Conservatoires in either London or Paris to further her studies with the flute. Cynthia sensed that the flute was a very important part of the girl's life and wondered how Jacques fitted in. She just couldn't see the relationship continuing beyond the end of the year when Tilly was due to leave. Tilly had also confided to Cynthia that her Mum had died the previous year and that her father wasn't handling the situation well.

On a recent visit, Tilly seemed to have something on her mind but Cynthia couldn't put her finger on it. Normally, Cynthia could wangle her conversations so that she found out all she wanted to. However, something certainly was wrong. Tilly normally appeared what Cynthia would describe as 'quietly confident'. However, the day of the questioning, she had appeared quite frazzled and slightly jumpy. She hadn't looked at all well and told Cynthia she had been fighting a severe stomach bug, something she said had been a result of something she'd eaten at the coffee shop. Cynthia also thought the girl had lost weight but decided not to mention this fact. She didn't know what to make of her. It was all a bit of a mystery.

Cynthia re-ran the recent conversation she had had with Tilly. It had gone along these lines, 'How're the flute lessons progressing?'

The response was a luke-warm, 'OK, thanks.'

Pushing for more information, Cynthia continued with, 'Have you heard from any of the Conservatoires you've applied to? Which one would you prefer, in London or Paris?'

Normally Tilly's hazel eyes would light up and her slightly freckled face would become animated. However, this time her answers lacked enthusiasm, 'Yes, I have got a place in London.'

'Congratulations! That's marvellous news. How wonderful for you! You must be so excited.' However, Tilly hadn't shared the enthusiasm and that was the end of the conversation.

When Cynthia had inquired if everything was alright, she'd replied, 'I'm fine, just tired. I have to go now,' and walked out rather abruptly.

'Well, I'll never get the job done if I stand here talking to myself,' sighed Cynthia to no one but herself, 'I suppose it'll sort itself out.'

Chapter 23

Since his first visit to the dogs' refuge with Stephie, Dan couldn't stop his thoughts drifting back to Scruffy. He kept thinking of the dog and wondering what had happened to him in a previous life for him to be found in such a sorry state. He couldn't wait for his next visit to the dogs' refuge. The second visit, Claudia greeted him with, 'What's brought you back so soon?'

'I thought I'd come to check up on Scruffy if that's alright with you?'

'No problems, but don't expect a miracle,' she responded with a slight glint in her eye and a wink to Stephie.

'You know where he is. In you go.'

Stephie looked at her, as Dan walked with determination towards the cage. 'I'm not so sure about a miracle. Just wait and see. I think the dog is having a positive effect on Dan which is something he needs. Let's see what happens.'

Dan slowed down his pace as he entered the dark cage. He bent low so as not to frighten the dog who was again cowering in the corner on his canvas bed. However, this time when Dan slowly lowered himself to sit, he positioned himself a little closer to the dog. He thought he noticed a look of recognition on the dog's face, accompanied by a slight raising of his head. Dan sat silently for the first 5 minutes before he began to whisper so as not to startle the dog.

'Hi Scruffy, I've come to see you again. How're you doing? Are you feeling any better? You are a good boy. You are a good dog,' he continued as he gradually shuffled closer to the dog.

At first, Scruffy viewed him with caution. He wasn't used to this. This softly spoken human made him feel warm and fuzzy although he was unable to put his feelings into words. Was he ready to trust? He wasn't sure. His doggy intuition told him to stay where he was and listen to the soothing words, which he was not able to understand, but which took away some of the hurt. He found he could tolerate the low calming noises Dan was whispering.

Scruffy knew he didn't like people with loud voices who had shouted at him in the past. Even worse, had been the fear he had felt when the hand of the human he had lived with had grabbed the big stick and had hit him. The pain had been beyond his doggy endurance. It had not just happened once but many times. He had lived in constant fear. It had been a welcome relief when he found himself being flung into the back of the filthy van and driven along bumpy tracks.

When the owner of the van had abruptly stopped the vehicle, had marched determinedly to the rear doors, flung them open and had grabbed him by the scruff of his neck, hauled him towards the back door and had flung him violently onto the gravel verge at the side of the road and had driven away, it was, in some ways a relief. Even though he was left cold, dirty, hungry and thirsty, it was preferable to staying in the abysmal surroundings which had been the only home he could remember.

But no one knew this. How could he ever describe what had happened?

All he knew was that he was in a happier place. Was he happy? Did he know what being happy was? When he had been found by the side of the road he hadn't much strength left to live. His initial relief at escaping from his previous owner had swiftly been replaced by fear. He was utterly scared and his whole body shook. He'd rather die than be taken to another home like the last one. He wanted to keep himself safe and the only way he knew how to do this was to lock himself inside himself, trusting no one, not letting anybody near him. Emotionally, he had shut down. Physically, he wasn't great. All that time without proper food was beginning to take its toll. Being thrown kitchen scraps wasn't food for a dog. Now, he was getting fed but he just couldn't be bothered to make the effort. He had lost the will to live – that was until this human they called Dan had appeared. Scruffy felt that he had something in common with this boy. He didn't under-stand the feeling .... so for now, he was content to sit in his corner and listen.

Dan continued his conversation until Stephie sauntered along to tell him it was time to go. Dan looked at the dog and said, 'Bye Scruffy. I'll come again as soon as I can.'

The dog picked up his ears for the first time as he watched Dan leave.

'I think you may be making some progress with Scruffy,' she told Dan.

His reply was, 'When can I come again?'

Stephie noticed his enthusiasm and replied, 'Soon. How about next weekend?' It was the first time since his Mum had died that she'd noticed he was taking an interest in something and for that she silently thanked Scruffy.

Chapter 24

GILLIE WAS AWARE OF THE RUMOURS CONCERNING TILLY. She'd heard snippets of conversation as she'd walked along the corridors of Grantham House. The senior girls huddled in groups of twos and threes had eyed her with suspicion and stopped talking as soon as she was anywhere near them. This was most unusual. Something was very wrong. Normally, they'd smile or ask her how she was.

She'd been keeping an eye on Tilly ever since the girl had returned to the Academy after her mother's death. She knew she was vulnerable and had taken the loss of her mother very hard.

However, Gillie, apart from being a Housemother also taught Song Writing at the Academy. She had lots of responsibility as Tilly wasn't the only student with problems. The girls knew her door was always open to them when they needed to chat about something. She was always welcoming and never turned anyone in need away. They usually left with a smile on their faces especially after sampling Gillie's chocolate cake.

This year had been particularly hectic as she was working with one of the new students, Amanda, who was in her first year at the Academy. She had been bullied at her previous school and although over it, she was adamant in setting up an anti-bullying support group. Amanda had the support of her best friend at the Academy, Immie, and Gillie had offered to give the girls support in setting up the group. This was taking up a lot of her spare time as they were organising fundraiser concerts. Gillie didn't mind this at all but it meant that she didn't have quite as much time as she normally would have done.

After being a Housemother at St C's for a few years, she well understood how the minds of teen girls worked. Once they had latched onto an item of news, it became their sole topic of conversation. She could never understand how they could talk around the subject for hours, building it up into such gigantic proportions. Usually, it was so exaggerated, it hardly resembled the original story at all.

The news of the argument in the lane had filtered through to her and she was well aware that Tilly's romance had come to an abrupt end. Everyone, even the younger students, appeared to be discussing it at great length. Gillie failed to understand why it was such hot news. Perhaps she was missing something. She scolded herself for not having sought out Tilly recently to find out how she was coping.

Her thoughts returned to the evening when she had witnessed Tilly's return from the village when she'd first met Jacques. She remembered how radiant Tilly had looked and she had felt so happy for her. Now she thought about it, she realised how little she'd seen of the girl during the last few weeks. Yes, she remembered seeing her on a few occasions skulking off in the direction of the practice rooms with her flute case tucked tightly under her arm. However, she didn't register it as being something to be overly concerned about. This was where Tilly normally escaped when things got too tough. Losing herself in her music was her way of coping. Overdoing it, Gillie had thought at the time. She had never considered following her, why should she?

But then the recollection of how sick Tilly had appeared when she'd last set eyes on her flashed before her. When she had inquired, Tilly had mentioned a gastric bug. She remembered advising the girl to visit the doctor. Surely she must be over that by now.

Chapter 25

AMY DIDN'T KNOW WHAT TO DO. SHE HAD NEVER BEEN IN a situation such as this. Tilly had begged her not to tell anyone. 'Promise me, you'll not tell anyone, please,' she'd beseeched her best friend. 'I couldn't live with myself if anyone found out.'

Amy felt the huge weight she was carrying around descend on her shoulders, her neck was stiff and a headache was brewing.

Tilly was expecting a lot from her. It wasn't certain that her friend was pregnant until she'd done a test. However, all the signs pointed towards it and if you looked at Tilly from a certain angle, she was sure she had thickened around the waistline and there was a hint of a bump. Of course, she'd heard of other girls becoming pregnant, but not at the Academy. Everyone there was so intent on becoming a professional musician that they wouldn't risk losing their place at such a prestigious establishment. She wouldn't admit to Tilly but she had been completely shocked by her best friend's news. Amy found it hard to believe. Tilly, of all people, to get herself in this fix. She was the sweetest girl who had had a rough time over the last few years. She didn't deserve this. Amy asked herself time and time again what she could do.

She decided to do what she always did when she was stressed and that was to phone her mum. Yes, she had made a promise to Tilly not to tell anyone, but this was too big a problem. The burden was too heavy for her to handle alone. She felt completely out of her depth. After a sleepless night, she decided to make the call. It wasn't as though her mum was at the Academy. Amy explained that she was asking for advice on behalf of a friend. Her mum, Pam, broke in, 'It's not Tilly is it?'

'I'm not supposed to be telling anyone, but I can't carry on any longer with a secret like this,' responded Amy with some relief attached to her voice. 'You won't tell anyone will you?'

Pam was shocked at the news. She had held a special place for Tilly in her heart as she had been close to Amy until recently.

She responded, 'No, I won't, but you're going to have to tell Gillie. You wouldn't be a good friend if you didn't. Tilly needs some help ... and the sooner the better. Let me know how you get on. Love you.'

'Love you too,' replied Amy. After ending the call, she thought about the last words, she had spoken. She whispered to herself, 'Poor Tilly will never be able to tell her Mum that she loves her.'

With a heavy heart, weighed down by lashings of guilt, Amy made her decision to visit Gillie that evening. It wasn't something she was looking forward to. However, she realised that something had to be done and the sooner the better for Tilly's sake.

Gillie watched Amy from her window in the flat which overlooked the path to the Music Block. She noticed that the normally vibrant student, who always blew everyone away with her enthusiasm for life, appeared distracted and had lost her bounce and enthusiasm. A few moments later, she saw her enter Grantham House and assumed she was making her way to her room on the second floor. Gillie decided to take matters into her own hands and stepped out into the corridor straight into Amy's path. Immediately she sensed she was the last person Amy wished to see. However, this was a conversation that she needed to have.

'Hi, Amy! How are you? Is everything OK? You look as though you have the worries of the world on your shoulders. I think we need to have a chat. I've time for a coffee or perhaps you'd prefer a hot chocolate, come along.'

Even though Amy had planned to speak to Gillie that evening, and had been rehearsing what she would say throughout the day, she was still apprehensive. However, deep down, she knew she had to have this conversation with Gillie. Even though she was dreading it, in some ways, she was relieved that Gillie had started the ball rolling.

When they arrived at the Housemother's flat Amy couldn't look Gillie in the eye. She felt she was betraying Tilly's trust. However, she need not have worried. Gillie was more perceptive than Amy gave her credit for. Realising the tension needed to be broken asked, 'Hot chocolate, latte or fruit juice?'

Amy gratefully accepted a hot chocolate whilst Gillie found the all-important ice-breaker, the tin containing the chocolate cake.

'Sit down. Don't look so worried. I'll begin the conversation shall I?' asked Gillie as she made herself comfortable on the settee opposite Amy.

'Yes, please,' replied Amy gratefully.

'I've got a feeling you're worried about someone?' Amy nodded. Gillie continued, 'This information is rather sensitive, am I right?'

Amy nodded again. 'I feel awful as I've promised that I'll not tell anyone but I've got to do something.'

Amy hunched her shoulders and fixed her eye on the rug in front of her.

'You don't have to tell me anything. Just answer with a yes or a no.'

Amy nodded in response.

'The problem lies with Tilly. Am I right?'

Again, Amy nodded.

'I'm not unobservant. I know she was seeing the guy from the village and that the romance appears to have ended.'

Amy nodded without looking at Gillie directly.

'I also know that Tilly hasn't been well. That she's been suffering from a so-called stomach bug which has taken a long time to settle. She's been avoiding me, and after inquiries, I know that she hasn't been to the doctor as I suggested. I'm going to come straight to the point. Do you think there's a chance she could be pregnant?'

With this, Amy burst into tears, which soon became heavy sobs. Gillie pushed a box of tissues towards her and waited. 'She asked me not to tell anyone,' she gulped wringing her hands together.

'But you haven't told me, I guessed,' she assured Amy. 'Don't worry. Leave it with me,' sighed Gillie. It wasn't a job she relished. Tilly was the last person she thought would have got herself into a fix like this.

After Amy had left, Gillie sat for quite a while wondering how she was going to handle the situation. What was the best way in which to approach Tilly? The girl had been through such a traumatic time. 'Such a shame,' she kept repeating. She was an exceptionally gifted student, not just as a flautist, but her academic grades were high. If this was true it was not only going to have a devastating effect on Tilly but upon her family. Tilly had given the impression that her father had almost become a recluse after his wife's death, shutting himself away in his home office and hardly venturing out except for work commitments and the odd shopping expedition. She had had a hard day. She decided she would 'sleep on it'. One night wouldn't make much of a difference to the situation.

Tilly was just about managing to keep up with all of her work commitments. It was easier now that the sickness had stopped. However, she realised that people were going to find out. She had lost weight due to the constant sickness. The fact that it was winter was in her favour. The lower temperatures meant that she could get away with wearing her windcheater so that when she began to show a more rounded tummy it wouldn't be quite so obvious. What she would do when she began to show, she shuddered to think.

She hadn't spoken to Amy since her recent meltdown and had buried herself in her studies. Being in her final year, meant she hadn't a fulltime academic timetable so she had found it easy to keep herself away from people and she spent most evenings in the single rehearsal rooms in the Music Block.

It was just as she was arriving back at her room after such a session that she saw Gillie waiting by her door. There was no way she could avoid her. It was obvious that Gillie knew. She only had to look at her, the sad expression and, the fiddling with the ring she always wore on her right hand. Tilly's stomach did a flip and she felt physically sick and began to shake.

'I think it's time for a coffee and a chat,' Gillie said kindly.

Tilly obediently followed the Housemother into her flat, like a lamb to the slaughter. In a way, she felt relief. Someone had to find out sometime but she fervently wished it was happening to someone else and not her.

The meeting wasn't going to be an easy one for either the Housemother or the student. Gillie had to be careful about how she approached the subject. Nothing was known at this point. However, it was obvious that something was very wrong. Tilly couldn't drink the coffee. She couldn't eat the biscuits. She just sat in a huddled position, arms clasped tightly around her stomach, sobbing. Gillie waited for Tilly to work through her anguish before attempting to speak to her.

In the end, Gillie didn't have to ask Tilly anything. It all came tumbling out in a rush. How she had been missing her mum and Jacques had come into her life and started to make her feel whole again. She knew she'd been stupid, although Gillie told her that she was not wholly to blame. There had been another person involved and that it sounded as though he had been the one to take advantage of her.

Afterward, Gillie said under her breath, 'I never, ever want to go through anything like that again.' It was heartbreaking to witness a confident, young woman disintegrate with such desperation, rocking backward and forwards on the settee. It reminded her of a caged animal, a free spirit that once had been so alive and vibrant and was now fragmented beyond repair.

Inevitably, Gillie insisted that Tilly must visit a doctor and that she was willing to accompany her. 'We need to know for certain if you are pregnant. We can't make any decisions until we know the facts,' she said gently. By this time Tilly had calmed down considerably. Gillie kindly said, 'Go to your room now and try to get some sleep. I'll talk to you in the morning.'

Chapter 26

Dan was becoming very worried. There were still no replies to his calls, texts or emails and his sister hadn't rung them on a Sunday evening for a few weeks now. What was going on? This wasn't like her at all. He'd mentioned it again to Stephie and she told him she hadn't had any luck with a response to her calls or texts either.

'Does your dad know anything?' she asked Dan. 'If it's anything serious, I'm sure the Academy would phone him. She just must be very busy.' However, Stephie didn't want to alarm Dan, but she was beginning to become concerned. It just wasn't like Tilly to cut herself off like this.

When Dan wasn't at school or busy doing his homework, he was at the dogs' refuge as Scruffy had become his number one priority. He could talk to the dog. Dan told him everything. On one of his recent visits, Stephie had suggested he take some treats into the cage to encourage the dog to respond and build a rapport with him. It wasn't long after this that Scruffy accepted a treat and he was now allowing Dan to pat and stroke his wiry coat. Dan felt he had won the lottery, when one day, he approached the gate of the cage and Scruffy had stood up, wagged his tail and walked towards him.

Now the pair had become warm friends and the relationship had graduated to Dan being able to take Scruffy for short walks into the bush area on the other side of the road to the refuge.

Dan had been hatching a plan for a few weeks now but he had kept it to himself. He wasn't sure how he was going to implement it or whether it would work. He was still calling round to Stephie's when he had the time. Being on the dog walking park with Stephie and Dizzy was one of his favourite places to be when he wasn't visiting Scruffy.

He had school friends but no one that close. He'd stopped inviting the gang of regular friends who had often frequented the house when his Mum had been alive. He'd kept in close contact with a couple of guys, Ben and Harry, who he'd been friendly with since he'd started school. He'd occasionally invited them around but the atmosphere was cold and unwelcoming. His Dad didn't help. If he was home he'd manage, 'Hi, how are you guys?' and disappear into his office before they'd even had a chance to reply.

When Jo had been alive, the house had always been full of activity and chatter. His friends had been warmly welcomed. His mum had been well known for her chocolate cake and there was always a freshly baked cake or biscuits to share when Dan's friends called in. She always showed such an interest in their lives and it was a joke that she almost knew them as well as their parents.

Life wasn't the same anymore. Dan thought that perhaps Ben and Harry would prefer not to come round to his place. Not that he ever asked them. He sometimes received invites to their homes for a meal for which he was grateful. Jo had been a popular member of the community. As she had taught at the local primary school she had been well known. However, there was this awful hole. His friends had Mums. Even the guys whose parents had split up didn't get it. They were still in contact with the parent who had left. His situation was different. He no longer had a Mum and he desperately wanted to hear from his sister.

Chapter 27

Gillie had dreaded taking Tilly into the city. The pregnancy test she had purchased on Tilly's behalf had shown the girl was pregnant. There was no doubt about it. Upon questioning Tilly on the date of her last period, Gillie ascertained she could be around sixteen weeks pregnant. Gillie was horrified, much further on than she had anticipated. She berated herself. Tilly had been under her care. How could she not have noticed? Now that she looked at Tilly, the oversized windcheater she was wearing was far too big for her slight frame and could easily be hiding a bump. Tilly urgently needed to see a doctor.

She'd offered to attend a clinic with Tilly in the city. It was the least she could do. Tilly had refused point-blank to have anything to do with the Academy doctor. The last couple of weeks had proven to be the most stressful Gillie had ever encountered. Thinking back, she found it hard to believe that as a Housemother of a girls' boarding house, she had never been confronted with a situation like this one before. Yes, she thought, there had been girls who had gone home for the holiday breaks and had not returned and no questions had been asked. She felt thankful that the girls of whom she was in charge had not put her in this difficult position before.

But Tilly was different. She acknowledged that the girl had been dealt a raw deal. Losing a mother at such a young age had been tough, especially after her mother had thought she had beaten the battle against breast cancer, only to have it return with such a vengeance. Then, there was her father. Gillie acknowledged his grief but to shut himself off like that without giving his daughter any support, seemed to Gillie, unforgivable. She was concerned about how he would take the news of his daughter's pregnancy but she would deal with that another day.

She couldn't blame the girl for her involvement with Jacques. She had needed someone to care for her and make her feel important. What girl would not be flattered by a gorgeous guy paying her so much attention? It was such a shame that he had treated her so abysmally. Perhaps if some of the girls had been upfront with her and had warned her, Tilly would not be in the position she now found herself. They all seemed to be aware of his motives in taking a girl out. She shuddered at this thought and wondered if he had tried it on with any of the other senior students. They all seemed aware of what he was like. It was a pity that he had picked on Tilly who had been so yearning for affection. She just wished she'd had the time to keep up with the village gossip. Perhaps she could have stopped this from happening. However, from the knowledge she had gained, she'd understood that Tilly had been infatuated with Jacques and probably would have resented any interference.

On discussing the problem with Chiara De Luca, whom she had sworn to secrecy, she'd been assured with a lot of waving of the arms and clinking of purple bracelets that she shouldn't blame herself. Chiara had said dramatically, 'It was just a tragedy waiting to happen.'

Not that this well-intentioned offering made Gillie feel any better. Her priority was to Tilly who had been so naive in some respects. All those years concentrating on her mum had probably meant she had missed out on the normal crushes that young teens experienced. Instead, desperate for someone to take a special interest in her and show her love and affection, she had fallen head over heels in love with the biggest scoundrel who only had one thing on his mind. It was such a shame. Now the deed had been done and it had to be sorted out.

To Gillie's relief, she had not had long to wait before obtaining an appointment for Tilly at a clinic in the city. The Housemother had done some research, made a few phone calls and hoped she had made the right decision. At Tilly's insistence, the doctor had to be a female. During the call to the clinic, Gillie had explained Tilly's situation and that, in her opinion, her student was in a delicate mental state and that the resulting stress was now causing frequent panic attacks witnessed by Gillie. Tilly had emerged from these with an ashen face, trembling and covered in perspiration. These episodes were of great concern to Gillie. The Housemother didn't like to admit that it would be a relief for her to pass the responsibility of Tilly's dilemma on to someone else.

She had asked herself numerous times whether it would have been better for Tilly to have had an abortion. Not that she agreed with them in general terms. It was all so complicated as Tilly was still unwilling to discuss the pregnancy with her in detail. Normally, a well-balanced girl, Tilly appeared to have adopted the idea that if she didn't acknowledge the pregnancy, it could still disappear. Gillie assumed Tilly would be going home to have the baby and then the situation and decision making would be out of Gillie's hands. What a mess it had turned out to be!

There were so many unanswered questions. Gillie had had to report the situation to Dr Hathaway, the Dean of the Academy, who had been utterly shocked. Having never married, the Academy was his life. Although excellent at his job under normal circumstances, anything irregular sent him into a frenzy. He had burst out with a barrage of questions of which Gillie failed to supply him with the answers. 'Of course, she'll have to leave the Academy!' he'd raged. 'She couldn't cope with the demands of the Academy and looking after a baby. We don't offer motherhood classes here!'

Gillie had known what his reaction would be. If Tilly had been attending another college, then perhaps things would have been different. Studying at the Academy was a fulltime commitment and, as the institution was private, the Dean had the final say on whether a student could continue with their studies.

'You're her Housemother, sort it out, sort it out,' he bellowed waving his arms in the air. 'Come and see me when it's sorted! The sooner the better, we have a reputation to uphold.'

No sympathy there, Gillie thought to herself as she returned, shaken to her flat.

Gillie had returned from the clinic with Tilly. The events had left both women in a daze. There had been so much to take in. For Gillie, never having been pregnant, it had been an eye-opener. For Tilly, it was the most embarrassing experience of her young life.

The first thing that Tilly had noticed when she had apprehensively entered the waiting room was that there was an air of expectancy. The other women, of differing ages, all appeared so happy and excited and most women were supported by their partners or their mothers. She felt that there was a great divide between herself and these other women. Sitting waiting for her appointment, she couldn't help but notice the walls which were covered with brightly coloured posters filled with information about the birthing process and newborn babies. There were pictures of chubby, healthy babies being cuddled adoringly by their mums. Piles of magazines littered a coffee table; again the covers illustrated nothing but happy Mums and babies. Thankfully, they were called in quickly and a somewhat sombre Tilly entered the doctor's consulting room.

Gillie had tried to warn Tilly saying, 'I expect there'll be lots of questions and an examination.' She noticed that Tilly instantly shuddered which was accompanied by a look of dread on her face. 'Would you like me to come in with you?' Gillie offered.

Tilly nodded.

Gillie could not help but admire Dr Blair, possibly in her late 30s, with an air of authority, but able to show empathy. Her caring attitude was obvious as she welcomed Tilly and made her feel as comfortable as possible. Gillie had pre-warned her of Tilly's fragile state. As this was Tilly's first visit, the consultation was, as expected, lengthy.

The time in Dr Blair's office appeared as a blur. There was so much to take in. Tilly answered the doctor's questions directly and clearly. However, the doctor did not fail to notice that the girl sitting in front of her appeared detached, almost as if she was discussing another person and that this baby was nothing to do with her. The doctor found this disconcerting and she tried to notice Gillie's reaction without Tilly being aware.

The first question, 'Do you know the date of your last period?'

Tilly replied defiantly, 'Yes. I've done nothing but count the days since then.'

'I've some more questions and then I'll examine you.'

There followed questions concerning Tilly's general health and her medical history as well as any physical symptoms that she was experiencing. The questions seemed endless. The doctor wanted to know if she was taking any medications. Her blood pressure was taken and she was sent out to the bathroom with a specimen jar and asked to return with a urine sample. She was weighed. Blood tests were arranged and so it went on.

Then it was time for her to be examined. This was the part Tilly had been dreading. She was aware that the doctor was feeling and measuring her tummy and then she was listening for the baby's heartbeat. It was decided that she should have an ultrasound done as she was so far on with the pregnancy. Phone calls were made to a radiological clinic in the same building and the pair was hustled along as there was an available time slot.

Up until then, Tilly was still secretly clinging onto the faint hope that perhaps the pregnancy was a huge mistake. She felt as though she was drowning deeper and deeper into the depths where she would suffocate with the knowledge she didn't want to acknowledge.

After the ultrasound that Tilly stoically underwent with Gillie sitting by her side and clasping her hand, there was a break of an hour. They visited the cafe on the ground floor and waited for the ultrasound results to be emailed to the doctor. Then they both returned to her rooms.

'Well, the good news is that your baby appears to be fine. It's in the correct position and possibly a little small but we can keep an eye on that. By all accounts, your baby should arrive by around the 20th December. How do you feel about that?' the doctor asked with a concerned expression.

Tilly fixed her eyes on a spot on the carpet and clasped her hands together. 'I don't want this baby,' she replied. 'It's going to ruin everything I've ever dreamed of. I hate myself for getting in this fix but I'll just have to live with it.'

'Have you considered having an abortion or giving up the baby for adoption?'

'No, it's not an option,' Tilly replied immediately. 'I can't do that. If Mum was here she'd never have forgiven me ... and I'd feel guilty for the rest of my life.'

There was a questioning look and Gillie shook her head in answer.

'Well,' the doctor replied. 'We'd better make sure this baby is going to be healthy.' She then discussed healthy eating and gave Tilly a leaflet issued by the Government Food Authority which listed all the foods that she could eat and a whole list of foods to avoid.

Then other instructions, such as no alcohol, smoking or taking drugs. Tilly looked at the doctor with such disdain and replied, 'As if I would!'

Gillie felt she had to but in and explain Tilly's rudeness. 'Tilly doesn't do any of those things.'

The doctor looked at Gillie in response and explained, 'But I have to warn her. It's my job.'

Gillie nodded meekly in response.

'Tilly, just wait outside in the waiting room, will you?'

When Tilly had departed, the doctor looked at Gillie and said, 'Tragic case. I expect she'll be going home to have the baby?'

'Her father hasn't been informed. That's a job for me this evening,' Gillie responded flatly.

'Well, let me know what's happening. I'll need to set up some support, a social worker, etc if she hasn't any support from home. I'll also need to discuss birth plans, antenatal classes, etc but that can wait a while. First of all, we need to know what's happening on the home front.'

'I'll keep you informed,' promised Gillie.

She left the rooms with a heavy heart and clutching leaflets and forms that listed dates for checkups, scans, etc as well as useful websites including Teen Pregnancy Forums and anything that might be of use in supporting the expectant Mum.

It was a very quiet drive on the return journey. Tilly sat huddled in the front seat of the car lost in her thoughts. It seemed as though she had disappeared into another world that was inaccessible to anyone but herself. Her fragile form and dazed expression were enough to bring tears to the Housemother's eyes. It was obvious that the girl was overwhelmed by the whole situation.

Tilly may have given the impression of being listless and limp like a rag doll, but her mind was, in fact, a hive of activity. Thoughts were whizzing around too fast for her to focus on one thing. It was all too much at that moment. She decided the best thing to do was to disassociate herself with the situation. She decided to take her thoughts back to an earlier period in her life when she'd been happy. She'd concentrate on that and nothing else. However, it was proving hard.

Throughout the journey, Gillie kept glancing sideways to view how Tilly was reacting in the passenger seat. She noticed the blank stare as though Tilly was somewhere else.

The Housemother had done some research, made a few phone calls and hoped she had made the right decision. During the call to the clinic, Gillie had explained Tilly's situation and that, in her opinion, her student was in a delicate mental state and was now suffering from frequent panic attacks witnessed by Gillie. Tilly had emerged from these with an ashen face, trembling and covered in perspiration. These episodes were of great concern to Gillie and she secretly feared for Tilly's mental health.

This isn't good, she thought to herself. She'd leave her be until she was closer to the Academy.

She still had to break the important news to the distraught girl that she couldn't stay on at the Academy. She had an idea that Tilly hadn't even considered that she would have to leave. She knew it wouldn't be taken well but decided it was better to tell her in the confines of the car rather than back at the Academy. She feared that Tilly could become hysterical and she didn't want everyone rushing forward to see what was happening. No, it couldn't wait. Gillie continued driving. She had a place in mind, the car park of a native animal reserve. She guessed it would be empty as the reserve closed early in the afternoon during winter. She was dreading telling Tilly the news.

Tilly showed the first sign of interest in her surroundings since leaving the clinic when Gillie turned left off the main road and braked on the gravel in the car park. She looked around, noticed that the car park was empty and the main gates to the reserve were locked. 'Why have we stopped here?' She turned to look at Gillie with a puzzled expression.

'I know you've had a terrible day and you've had enough information to absorb to last you a lifetime, but I've stopped here because I have something important to say and I thought it would be easier here than back at the Academy.'

Tilly looked at her as though she couldn't believe there was anything more awful for her to cope with.

Gillie noticed the apprehension written across Tilly's face, the biting of her bottom lip and the twisting of the ring on her right hand. It said it all. Gillie felt as though she was the wicked witch. What she was going to tell Tilly would blow her world apart even further. Her heart was already fragmented. Gillie knew she didn't have a choice. Before her eyes, flashed the recent conversation, if you could call it that, she had had with the Dean of the Academy. There had been no room for negotiation. It had been an ultimatum.

Gillie had left the clinic in a very low mood. Now that there was no question concerning the pregnancy, she had no option but to inform Tilly of the Dean's decision. His words had made it quite clear. 'There is no room here for a student who is expecting a child,' he'd stated.

Gillie had been instructed to impart this information. 'It's your job as her Housemother to tell her,' he'd bellowed.

After an uncomfortable silence, Tilly said, 'Well go on. It can't be anything worse than what I've already heard today.' On looking at Gillie's expression, she asked timidly, 'Can it?'

'I'm sorry I have to tell you this. You do realise, that under the present circumstances, you won't be allowed to continue studying at the Academy?'

Tilly's face had disbelief written all over it. When there was no immediate response from Tilly, Gillie continued. 'You do understand how difficult it would be for you to continue with your studies at the Academy? There would be no facilities there for a baby.'

With still no response, Gillie continued, not quite sure how much of this Tilly was taking in. 'We can arrange for your academic work to be sent to you at home. You'll be able to complete the assignments which you can then email or post to the college which deals with Distance Education. In this way, you'll still be able to complete your final year studies.'

Gillie realised that it was the word, *home*, which set about the panic attack. To her horror, she watched as, in an instant, Tilly had grabbed hold of the car door handle, flung open the door and threw herself out of the car. Gillie was thankful they were stationary. It was good that she had chosen a safe spot to park. She watched as the girl stamped and paced up to the entrance to the locked park gates, clung onto the gates for dear life trying to shake them open with all her might. It was as though the opening of the gates would relieve her of all her trauma. When this didn't happen, Tilly strode backward and forwards in front of the gate with her arms folded tightly across her chest. Gillie could almost feel the pent up emotion emanating from the girl. She knew it was no good getting out of the car at that moment. There was too much turmoil boiling and swirling through Tilly's body. Gillie just hoped and prayed this would not have too much of an effect on the unborn child.

She would stay in the car and wait whilst making sure that Tilly was safe. She watched as Tilly stopped the pacing and graduated to banging her head with her fists before she sank on the nearby grass and howled. The sound pierced through the air. Gillie's first thoughts were of a caged animal. She almost expected the animals in the reserve to join in with their various calls of distress. Heavy sobbing replaced the howling. Gillie was horrified. She had never experienced anything like this before. Springing into action, she quickly stepped out of the car and ran across to Tilly wrapping her in a huge bear hug and holding her tightly until the worst had passed.

When her sobs gradually subsided, Gillie decided enough was enough for one day and said, 'Come on, get in the car. What we need is a cup of tea.' With a promise from Tilly that she wouldn't do anything stupid like jump out of the car, they set off. Nothing more was said. Both of them had too many things on their minds.

Gillie spent the rest of the journey tossing around in her mind whether to continue discussing future arrangements that night back at the Academy or leave it until the morning. She needed to complete her task but asked herself whether Tilly was able to take any more stress that day.

This question was answered back in her flat. Tilly sat huddled in the armchair clutching her mug of tea and gazing into space, her expression, hopeless. Gillie thought how lost and forlorn Tilly appeared. How she wished she could wave a magic wand and make it all better. No, she decided to leave the remainder of her talk until the next day.

'Off you go and try to sleep,' Gillie said kindly. She was also desperate for her bed but doubted very much that she would have a good night. As Tilly walked towards the door, she turned to look at Gillie and said, 'Thanks for coming with me. I don't know what I would have done without you.'

This brought Gillie almost to tears. She had a soft spot for this girl. She couldn't condone what she had done, but it now needed to be sorted in the best way possible.

'Come and see me tomorrow morning,' she replied. She watched with anguish, as one of the most promising students the Academy had ever had, walked out of her flat. How she wished that Tilly's pain could be washed away. But, it wasn't that simple.

Chapter 28

Gillie had no choice. She was the one who had been instructed to break the news to Tilly's father. She dreaded the thought but it had to be done. It was only fair to inform Tilly before she took any action. She was not looking forward to the task ahead.

When Tilly arrived at the flat the next morning, it was obvious that the girl hadn't slept a wink. Normally, neat as a pin, Tilly arrived with not an ounce of colour on her face. Her makeup, carefully applied to conceal the dark circles underneath her eyes, failed to hide her pallor. Gillie's thoughts on seeing the girl in the light of day were that she felt as bad as Tilly looked. 'Come on in. Sit down,' she said patting a cushion and trying to be as normal as she could be. 'Coffee? Tea?'

'I think I'd prefer a glass of water, if you don't mind,' responded Tilly as she sat gingerly on the edge of the seat indicating to Gillie that she felt uncomfortable in the situation.

Now seated, Tilly clutching onto her glass of water nervously with both hands, and Gillie holding onto a hot mug of coffee, and hoping the caffeine would give her the courage which she needed, she broached the subject she was dreading.

'I know yesterday was a very stressful day for you. However, there are some other things I need to discuss with you. You do realise that your dad has to be informed of the situation?'

Tilly froze. Gillie thought the glass Tilly was grasping would shatter into tiny fragments if she continued to hold it so intensely. Gillie gently unfolded her fingers from around the glass and placed it on the coffee table in front of her.

'Does he have to know? He'll kill me!' exploded Tilly.

'Well, no, not by law, but I can't see how you can cope if you don't tell him. You'll need support for yourself and the baby and home would be the best place.'

Tilly's reply came loud and strong, 'I can't go home. I won't go home!' She was now striding from one side of the room to the other with hands clenched tightly together.

Gillie feared for a repeat outburst similar to the one of the previous day. This wasn't good for either Tilly or the baby. She gently coaxed Tilly into a sitting position. Nothing was to be gained by all this emotion.

Gillie prayed that the right words would come to her. 'Have you any thoughts about what you'd like to do? I take it the relationship between you and Jacques is over?'

'I can't go home. Dad would never forgive me. Jacques is the last person I want to see. I wish I'd never met him. If I hadn't met him, I wouldn't be in this fix. Abortion isn't an option. Life sucks.'

'Well, what do you think about me telling your dad?'

After a moment of hesitation, Tilly nodded. By now the silent tears were running down her face and the tissue she was grasping was sodden.

Handing a box of tissues which Gillie always kept on hand, she said, 'Here, take as many tissues as you need. Just let it out – all that emotion. No one can hear.' She sat quietly by the grief-stricken girl until there were no more tears. 'I'll ring him this evening. Until then, try not to worry. I'll let you know what he says.'

Tilly was by now standing. She was shaking her bent head from side to side and said, 'I know what he'll say.' With that she turned and walked out of the flat, leaving the Housemother wishing desperately for an answer to the present problem. Feeling distraught, she said, 'What a mess, so sad for this to happen to Tilly, life just isn't fair.'

Fortunately, it was nearly the end of the semester and an ideal time for Tilly to go home as usual for the break, but, of course, to not return. It took an enormous amount of courage for Gillie to phone Tilly's father that evening. She had anticipated shock, being upset, unacceptance, disappointment, anger even. However, she had not anticipated the outrage and disgust with Pete's response to the news.

'Good evening, Mr Morgan. I'm sorry to disturb your evening but I have some news regarding Tilly that I must share with you.'

'What's the matter with her? Is she ill? I can't take any more bad news!'

'Well, I'm afraid you're not going to like what I have to tell you. Tilly is not ill. However, yes, she does have some issues concerning her health.'

'What do you mean? What issues?'

'Tilly is going to have to leave the Academy at the end of this term. She's very distressed about the situation.'

'What situation?' he blared.

'There's no easy way to tell you this, but Tilly is pregnant.'

'Pregnant! You must be mistaken. I've left her in your care and you're telling me, she's pregnant. Not Tilly! She wouldn't do such a thing.'

'I'm afraid it's true.'

'NO!' he boomed.

By now, Gillie was distressed beyond words. Tilly's father was making her angry and she was pacing around her tiny flat. 'Mr Morgan, your daughter has been grief-stricken ever since she lost her mother. She has been like a lost soul.'

'How do you think I've been feeling? What are you trying to tell me, that I've not been grieving as well?'

'Please Mr Morgan, let me finish. Of course, I understand your family situation and I realise that losing your wife was heartbreaking for all of you. However, let me finish. Tilly has not coped well with losing her mother. If I might add, she has received little support from home. She met a guy from the village. At first, he was charming and caring and he was the one she felt a rapport with, someone she could confide in. I have never seen her look so happy. However, Tilly underestimated him and he took advantage of her vulnerability.'

'Well, I'm pleased to hear she's found someone to make her so happy. She can stay with him for all I care. I don't want her darkening my doors here. She's not welcome. She can stay with him. This would have broken her mother's heart ... and she's ruined her career. What a disgrace!'

With those words piercing the airways, he ended the call.

Gillie was left shaking and in a state of shock. Now she fully understood why Tilly had flatly refused to go home. She didn't blame the girl.

The news that he had refused to have Tilly return to the family home was something Gillie had not even considered. Tilly couldn't stay at the Academy that was for sure. That night Gillie did not sleep a wink.

Chapter 29

To say that Cynthia was upset was an understatement. To say that she was hurt, devastated even, and so, so angry would have been closer to the mark. To find, on calling Jacques down for dinner the previous evening, and upon receiving no answer, she had knocked on his door and on entering his room had found to her dismay that all of his gear had disappeared. She flung open his wardrobe door and was aghast to find it empty except for some really old jeans. In desperation, she attacked the drawers and with furthering panic, found them to be also empty.

On first thoughts, her mind sprang to the fact they'd had burglars, but then she'd noticed the envelope propped up in a prominent position on his bedside table. She could hardly contain herself and her fingers were fumbling with apprehension as she tore it open. She couldn't believe what she read. He'd left, the note said, and now had a job in the city. He told her not to search for him and he'd be in touch.

'What does it mean?' she cried in anguish as she thrust the note into her husband's hand when he arrived home from work a few moments later. 'What have we done wrong?'

'We haven't done anything wrong except spoil him and let him run away from his responsibilities. There's talk in the village about him and just about every girl who lives around here. I heard some gossip from the local guys. They didn't realise who I was. And before you ask, no, I'm not telling you what they said. Don't worry; he'll come back when he needs more money.'

Cynthia couldn't eat her dinner, she couldn't settle. Her husband, frustrated with her continuous tirade against her son, had left half of his dinner uneaten and had stormed out of the kitchen and made his way to his refuge, the shed at the bottom of the garden. She heard him slam the shed door and knew there was no point in following him. He'd always told his wife, the shed was his domain, a place of refuge to where he escaped when he needed some peace and quiet.

She spent the rest of the evening walking aimlessly from room to room. She tried to phone Jacques, but the call was not answered. 'How could he do this?' she asked repeatedly. She had known for a while now that something was wrong. She had tried to talk to him, to ask him if there was a problem but he always walked out. She knew he'd packed in Tilly and she wasn't stupid. She also knew he'd been seen hanging around with at least one other girl. The village gossipmongers had been at work. However, she didn't want to know what people were saying. He was still her son, her only child and she loved him.

Chapter 30

DAN WAS ENGROSSED IN HIS FAVOURITE TV SHOW AND didn't hear the landline extension ring in his father's study. However, he certainly heard the conversation that followed. He immediately knew something was wrong, very wrong and it was to do with his sister. He heard his dad shouting in rage. He then heard him shout, 'Pregnant!' In disbelief he said out loud, 'She can't be, not Tilly!' Dan's world came to a halt. Tilly! Pregnant! No. She wasn't that sort of a girl. Not his sister. She was going to study at the Conservatoire. Nothing would stop her from doing that.

His father continued to rant and rave. His words became louder and Dan could hear him pacing the floor in his study. Dan heard the general gist. The Academy was blamed, Gillie was blamed. It was when Dan heard his dad say that Tilly was not to come home, that it hit him. She had done the deed and she could go to live with someone called Jacques who made Tilly so happy. She had ruined her wonderful chances. The shame and so it continued. That was why he hadn't heard from his sister for weeks. He had known something was wrong.

Dan didn't approach his father. He knew it wasn't the right time. After the phone call, he could hear his father's rants continuing and what sounded like heavy books being thrown onto the floor and for some reason, furniture being moved. He then heard Pete open the drinks cabinet and knew he was reaching for the whisky bottle. This was becoming a regular occurrence since his mum had died.

He left everything and ran out of the house, banging the front door behind him. He knew his dad wouldn't notice his absence for a while. Once the whisky took hold, he'd be dead to the world. There was no point in him going to bed. He wouldn't sleep. He knew he wouldn't. There was too much on his mind. How many more traumas could he survive? There was one place he knew he could go. Even though it was getting late, Stephie would understand. Her home was his sanctuary, his haven.

Recently, he'd hatched a plan. With a heavy heart and resentment, he realised it would have to be put on hold. It was something that had made him feel better in himself, something that had given him some hope and joy. He'd kept it a secret. Now, he realised it wasn't the right time to approach his father. He knew how he would respond to anything that might disrupt the house at the moment.

Now he understood the reason why Tilly had shut

herself away from everyone, the lack of calls, the unanswered texts, all made sense. A part of him felt great compassion. He knew his sister. He knew that behind all of this something wasn't right. The last thing she would do would have been to get pregnant. However, another part of him felt so angry. This was going to upset everything.

Chapter 31

As soon as Dan burst through the front door, Stephie knew something was dreadfully wrong. He was out of breath, having, Stephie assumed, run straight down to her house. Her first thought was that there must have been some sort of emergency with Pete. Had he collapsed? He'd certainly been under a lot of strain. She felt weak as a wave of nausea washed through her body landing in the pit of her stomach like a dead weight.

But no, perhaps she'd got it wrong. Dan was angry, so angry. She could feel the tension as he refused to sit down and with hands clenched he repeatedly paced the small living room. The situation was made worse by Dizzy who had instantly honed into the situation and had joined in the pacing whilst barking loudly.

With Dizzy banished to her bed, Stephie demanded, 'Tell me, Dan. Tell me what's wrong?'

'She's pregnant!' muttered Dan in disgust.

'Who is?'

'Can't you guess? My stupid sister, that's who!' yelled Dan.

Stephie's reaction was one of shock and she grabbed onto the nearest chair and lowered herself down. 'No, not Tilly. You must have made a mistake. I can't believe it.'

'I wish it was a mistake. I hate her. She's messed up everything. Dad said she can't come home. He never wants to see her again.'

'Dan you need to calm down. I can't make sense of this. Tilly wouldn't get herself pregnant. She's got too much to lose with her career. Sit down and I'll go to make a cup of tea or would you prefer a soft drink? I've got some Coca Cola.'

'Water will do,' he responded with an impatience that Stephie knew was due to stress.

'Well, I think I need coffee,' she replied.

Whilst she filled the kettle and switched it on, and reached for the tin of biscuits she knew were Dan's favourites, she had an awful feeling that the story may have some truth to it. Tilly had gone through so much with very little support. Pete had been so consumed with grief; he'd withdrawn into himself and had not been there for his daughter. Neither Dan nor herself had heard from Tilly for a while which was very unusual. She was filled with love, concern and a certain amount of fear for her late friend's daughter. She remembered the promise she had made to Jo before she had died that she would be there for Tilly and she felt sick with failure.

When Stephie returned from the kitchen, carrying the tray containing a plate of biscuits, one glass of water and two mugs of coffee, in case Dan changed his mind, she found him sobbing uncontrollably and trying hard to stop the flow of tears by covering his face with a soaking tissue. She put the tray down on the coffee table and knelt in front of the chair where he was sitting. 'I'm here for you,' she whispered to the distraught young man. He raised his head, looked at her and flung his arms around her neck. They stayed like this until his tears had subsided.

'Come on, tell me all about it. Start at the beginning,' Stephie said gently.

Dan relayed the whole story. It was a relief to be able to off-load.

'I didn't mean what I said earlier,' he whispered. 'I don't hate Tilly. It's just that I had plans and now I don't know whether they'll work out,' he said.

'Do you want to tell me about the plans?' Stephie asked him tentatively.

'No, not yet,' he replied.

'Well, let's see if we can find out more information. We're skating on thin ice at the moment. Perhaps it's time you went home. Your father will wonder where you are.'

'He won't, he doesn't care,' said Dan, shaking his head. 'He's probably still ranting and raving about Tilly or he's fallen asleep after drinking the whisky. It's late so I suppose I'd better go.'

'I'm always here. Try to sleep,' was Stephie's response.

It was going to be a long night. She knew she wouldn't be able to sleep.

Chapter 32

EVER SINCE JACQUES HAD DEPARTED IN SUCH A HURRY, Cynthia had known something was wrong, not just a little niggly thing but something serious. She had not been able to focus on anything. Now there was the phone call of the previous evening to consider. This had heightened her level of apprehension. She felt she couldn't take much more.

Cynthia noted the seriousness of the tone in Gillie's voice. The stiff introduction said it all. 'Good Evening Mrs King. It's Gillie Longhurst. I'm one of the Housemothers from St C's. I hope you are well. I wonder if you are free tomorrow afternoon. I'd like to call round with Tilly.'

There was a formality about the call. It wasn't just her and Tilly calling round for a casual chat and a cup of tea. A definite time had been arranged. Why would the Housemother, whom Cynthia had never met before, request half an hour of Cynthia's time?

Cynthia's husband had tried to calm his exuberant wife down. You only had to mention something to her and it had a habit of spiralling up into something huge. A visit couldn't be just a visit. It had to be a visit about something very important and Cynthia appeared to have an imagination with supersonic powers. She had been putting two and two together and the answer certainly wasn't four. She was well aware that the relationship between Tilly and her son had come to an abrupt halt a while ago. She had gleaned from village gossip that Jacques had been seen with other girls. The last time she'd seen Tilly, the girl had mentioned that the relationship between her and her father was at boiling point. She couldn't help but notice how sick the girl had appeared. She was positive she knew what this visit was all about. How her husband could think it was just a social call was beyond her. Men!

Tilly was apprehensive about the visit arranged by Gillie. She was well aware of Gillie's plan even though the Housemother hadn't voiced her thoughts concerning the matter. It didn't take much to think it out logically. After all, where was she going to live if she couldn't stay at the Academy and going home was completely out of the question?

She had long ago realised that her and Jacques' relationship had been based on one thing and she was disgusted that he'd used her in that way and left her in the lurch, homeless and destitute.

Cynthia busied herself all morning. She was up at 6 o'clock and had already started polishing the furniture in the living room before Derek had left to go to work.

'Cynth, they are only coming for a chat. It's not the Queen coming you know,' he joked.

'There's more to this than meets the eye. This visit isn't a joke. I feel it in my bones. It's something serious. Just you wait and see.'

Derek left the house to walk down the front path towards the garage, 'Something serious! I bet!' He smiled to himself. 'Why do women always make mountains out of molehills?' he chuckled.

It was now half-past two and Cynthia had worked herself into a frenzy. She had cleaned the house from top to bottom and had baked some cupcakes which she'd iced to look like flowers. The coffee table was set with tiny plates with matching cups and saucers and the cupcakes were displayed on fancy doilies on the 3 tier cake stand she'd inherited from her mother and which was only brought out on very special occasions. She'd toyed with the idea of whether to just set it up casually on the breakfast bar using mugs as she would if her neighbours called round. However, on reflection, she had decided, that as she considered this, to be a more formal event she needed the best china to match the occasion.

When she saw Tilly, accompanied by the Housemother, approaching the front gate leading into the tiny native garden that she tended with so much care, she stopped in her tracks. She knew it! Tilly looked dreadful. She had lost weight since she had last called round. She noticed Tilly's pale face with its dull complexion, her huge brown eyes below which there were telltale dark circles, the lank hair that needed a cut-and-blow. She noticed the lack of life and vitality and the look of defeatism on the girl's face. Then there were the drooping shoulders and the fact that her arms were crossed tightly in front of her body, hands clenched together hiding a small bump only just visible if someone was staring at her baggy windcheater.

Cynthia was at the door in a flash. Before Gillie had reached the front door, it was flung open and the small dumpty figure had flung herself out into the garden, had almost pushed Gillie unceremoniously out of the way and had flung her arms around Tilly who appeared uncomfortable being ensconced in a bearhug.

'Come inside love and sit down. I think we have lots to talk about, don't you? You too,' she said not quite sure how to address the Housemother.

'Please call me Gillie,' she responded to Cynthia's uncertainty.

'And I'm Cynthia,' she responded.

Cynthia led them into the sitting room. 'I'll put the kettle on and we'll have a cup of tea. Make yourself at home,' Cynthia said as she looked across at Tilly who was still standing frozen to the spot. This isn't going to be easy she thought as she left Gillie to attend to the frightened young woman who was a shadow of her former self.

It wasn't an afternoon that Gillie ever wanted to repeat. It proved uncomfortable, stressful as well as emotional. Cynthia didn't need to be told what the problem was. However, her emotions fluctuated between compassion for Tilly and anger at her son. However, the outcome was better than anticipated. Gillie had not needed to plead her case. She had spent an agonising evening racking her brain for an alternative home for Tilly. It was with relief that when Cynthia heard how Tilly's father had refused to have anything to do with her, she had immediately offered the girl a home. When Gillie had enquired, 'Perhaps you need to discuss this first with your husband before making a decision?'

Cynthia had immediately responded, 'No, no, he'll be fine about it. It would be great to have a baby in the house again.'

Gillie's prayers had been answered. Perhaps it was not the perfect answer, but the best one available at that moment.

Deep inside, Jacques' Mum was quite excited about becoming a grandmother and this was easing the situation. It was agreed that Tilly would remain at the Academy until the end of the semester and instead of going home, would move in with Jacques' parents. The students would assume she'd gone home as normal. It wouldn't take long before the truth was known as Tilly would still be in the area. Gillie had arranged for her to continue her weekly flute lessons at the Academy with her tutor, Jack Ford, but that was as far as her links went with St C's. She could also continue her academic work as a Distance Education student.

Tilly didn't know how she felt. The immediate problem had been fixed. She had a roof over her head, food and a warm bed but as far as long term plans, she didn't have any. She couldn't see a future for herself.

Chapter 33

TILLY LOOKED AROUND THE ROOM WITH A GLAZED expression. It was as though she had moved to another planet. Her world as she knew it had been completely turned around. The room, which had been offered by Cynthia, and for which she was thankful, was a mass of frills. They were everywhere, around the dusky pink pillowcases and surrounding the edges of the multi-coloured patchwork quilt. The white painted shelves were covered with knickknacks that had been collected over the years, obviously souvenirs from past holidays and gifts that had meaning to Cynthia but no one else. Faded framed prints covered the wallpapered walls. There was no way Tilly could personalise this room. She felt totally out of place. A few nights staying in such a room would have been possible but to live in here permanently? She was trying to estimate how long she would be able to put up with the situation. Her mind dramatically searched for alternatives. With a jolt, reality hit her hard. There was no alternative. She would have to stay here and make the best of a bad situation.

Her thoughts turned to home. Since her father's outburst and total rejection, she had only spoken to Dan once. He had appeared angry. It was the last thing she needed, especially from her brother. She didn't need people rubbing salt into the wound. She knew she was partly to blame for the situation she now found herself in. She couldn't feel any worse than she did already.

What she couldn't do was speak to Stephie. No way! She was so ashamed of herself. She was aware that Stephie had been in contact with Gillie and that she had sent her love. Tilly had responded with, 'Does she know where I am?'

Gillie had replied, 'Yes, I hope you don't mind but I thought someone ought to know.'

Tilly found it difficult to express how she felt. She had always opened up to her mum and they had been able to chat nonstop for ages. That option was closed. Now, she felt completely isolated. Cynthia just didn't understand her and she had no one else to talk to.

What no one understood was that since leaving the Academy, she had lost her identity. She was no longer a budding world flautist. She no longer had a place at the Royal School of Music in London. She no longer had a family. She had lost herself and with it, she had lost her self-esteem and her confidence. All her hopes and dreams had been washed away in a river of tears.

Without Cynthia's offer of a home, she didn't know what she would have done or where she would have ended up. She would be eternally grateful to Cynthia for taking her in and providing her with a roof over her head. However, the situation was difficult. She had learnt that Jacques had disappeared to live with his new girlfriend and said he would not return to the family home while Tilly was there with 'that brat'. This, in itself, created stress. Cynthia was livid with him but he was still her only son and she missed him.

Cynthia was trying her best. She had encouraged Tilly to use the house as though it was her home but she couldn't. It was all so different. They were like chalk and cheese. Cynthia was the kindest, most loving person but she was the total opposite to Tilly's Mum. Cynthia overflowed with fussiness which at times could become unbearable. The cottage was filled with fanciness, ornaments filled every nook and cranny, framed photos covered the walls and every chair was filled to overflowing with cushions of different patterns and hues.

She was ecstatic about becoming a granny. To this day, Tilly had been afraid to admit to Cynthia that she didn't want this baby. Her incessant baby chatter sometimes was just too much for Tilly who would suddenly leave the room in floods of tears. Cynthia would try to commiserate and blame this behaviour on the dreaded hormones and would fuss even more making matters twice as bad.

Her husband, Derek, would often have to step in.

'Cynth, give the girl some space. She's not used to all of this fussing,' he'd plead.

Tilly had been known to withdraw into her room for hours and spend time playing haunting melodies on her flute. It was the only time she could switch her thoughts off from her present situation.

'I don't mind her playing that instrument,' Cynthia would complain, 'but I wish she'd play something more up to date, something more cheerful.'

'You don't understand her,' commented her husband.

'I know she doesn't want this baby,' she stated. 'I don't understand a pregnant woman not wanting her child,' she said emphatically. 'She's not said anything. She doesn't need to.'

'Well, that's where you differ love,' her husband sighed. 'She wouldn't be having this baby if our son had shown her some respect. She'd have been making plans to study overseas. She's lost her mum and the rest of her family, she needs some understanding.'

Cynthia shrugged her shoulders and sighed, 'I suppose you're right. At least she's not had an abortion. I don't know what Jacques would have thought about that.'

Derek didn't immediately voice his opinion on the matter. He kept his thoughts to himself but secretly thought his son would have been relieved if Tilly had decided to terminate the pregnancy. 'What a thing to say,' responded Derek mystified at his wife's comment.

'Well, she could have done, couldn't she? She's been very emotional about it all. The doctor could have arranged it if she didn't think she was stable.'

'Cynthia, don't say things like that. She's not unstable. It's just that she is finding her present situation difficult. She said right from the beginning that she would have the child. She told us that it had been something her mum had instilled in her ... that abortion was the wrong thing to do, well the wrong thing for her to do. Just drop it.'

Chapter 34

DAN CONTINUED HIS VISITS TO THE DOGS' REFUGE WITH Stephie. It was the highlight of his week. Scruffy's trust in Dan had grown and he was now taking the dog out on walks whenever he visited. Dan had recently purchased a new collar and lead for the dog which he used when he took Scruffy out. Off came the tatty old brown leather collar which was replaced by the bright red shiny leather one. The dog had become more confident and had begun to show Dan his true character which he saved for Dan's visits. He sensed when it was Dan's visiting day. No longer did he sit hunched in the corner of the cage. He now had the confidence to venture out into the exercise yard where he could be found waiting expectantly at the gate. This only happened on the days when Dan was due to appear and none of the kennel staff could work out how he seemed to know that Dan was on his way.

After greeting his friend with great excitement, Scruffy's tail would wag madly from side to side and this was accompanied by squeaks of pure joy. Scruffy would sit obediently whilst the collar was changed, the lead clipped on and off they would go. Claudia commented, 'That boy and dog were made for each other. They both need each other so much and the magic is beginning to work. I knew it would. We just had to wait for the right moment.'

Stephie nodded in agreement. 'There's still a way to go for Dan and this business with his sister being pregnant isn't helping.'

'No hopes of her coming home then? That's where she should be in my opinion.'

Stephie, trying to hold back the tears, responded with, 'Yes, I agree, but Pete flatly refuses to see her at the moment. I can't imagine what Jo would have said if she knew of the situation. I feel as though I've let her down.'

Claudia, with arms crossed in front of her ample bosom, took on a stance of being in charge, responded with, 'Don't feel guilty. You've not let her down. That Jacques is the one who has let her down. Shame she ever met him. It was just a series of unfortunate events that all came together. Not your fault.'

With that, she left Stephie to ponder on the significance of her words. It was true; a vision of falling dominoes came before her. However, she felt that had Tilly received more support from her father when she had returned to the Academy, then the story may have had a different ending.

Chapter 35

It was now August and it was growing hard to not notice Tilly's bump. She was still thin and pale and was certainly not blooming. Since arriving at Cynthia's she had kept herself busy with her studies of her academic work and her music as well as attending appointments at the clinic.

She felt quite isolated as she had had almost no contact with any of the students from the Academy. Deep down she missed them. The more Tilly thought about it, she realised that whenever she'd walked through the grounds to the Music Block, the girls she'd seen had either turned away from her or offered snide comments and yelled out names that she couldn't repeat. The situation had made her feel physically sick and she'd been considering cancelling her lessons. Much as she enjoyed them, it wasn't worth the humiliation.

Even Amy had turned her back on Tilly when she had seen her in the Academy grounds as she was on her way to her weekly flute lesson. Tilly had called, 'Amy!' hoping that her friend would turn around.

'It's too complicated,' was all the reply she got.

When she had arrived home she had felt despondent and depressed and had reported the story to Cynthia, who had replied with, 'It's probably due to peer pressure love. Perhaps she didn't have a choice. Don't forget she has to live with those girls.'

Until now, it had always been the highlight of her week to spend time with Jack Ford. Now that the pregnancy was advancing and the bump was growing larger, the lesson was beginning to be stressful. Although Jack Ford had at first been shocked to learn of her pregnancy, he had tried to hide his feelings and to be empathetic to the situation. However, their relationship had altered. He felt he had to distance himself from Tilly. She was still his student but he couldn't quite get his head around the pregnancy. To tell the truth, although he would not admit it out loud, he was so disappointed in her. Ever since she had first arrived at the Academy, he had realised her potential. She had been his star pupil, his shining light. She was brilliant and it had always been a joy to nurture her talent. He had been so looking forward to following her progress after she'd left the Academy. Now that all hopes of continuing her studies overseas had been dashed, the spark between them had died. He didn't know what to say to her anymore.

Tilly's social life, if you could call it that, revolved around medical appointments which were becoming more frequent. She had little contact with anyone from the village and picked up most of the local gossip from Cynthia who was a lifeline to the outside world. Cynthia didn't agree with Tilly's decision to isolate herself. It wasn't her way. She realised there was a problem with the Academy girls but had tried, without success, to get Tilly involved in various events in the village.

Tilly had followed a few groups for Young Mums she'd found on Facebook. This didn't last for long before she gave up. The comments from other group members firmly reinforced that she was in a different league to the rest. Tilly wasn't a snob but she found that she had little in common with the other girls. Rather than supporting her, it accentuated her desperate plight and made her more depressed than ever.

Recently she had started to wear a drab brown billowing dress much to Cynthia's annoyance. Tilly had ordered it from an online shop and the drab colour seemed to symbolise her dark moods. She would cover her head with an enormous floppy straw sun hat and her eyes with dark-framed sunglasses with the hope that no one would recognise her.

That afternoon, she had needed to post an assignment and found two of the younger Academy students delivering posters for a fundraising concert. She recognised the two girls, Amanda and her friend, Immie, as they were quite well known in their efforts to start an anti-bullying support group at the Academy. When Tilly entered the post office she had every intention of dealing with her mail and leaving. However, the girls both smiled at her and said, 'Hi! How are you?'

Before she'd had time to respond, Immie continued with, 'We're going to the coffee shop before we return to the Academy. Have you time to join us?'

Instantly, Tilly replied, 'I'd love to. It's so kind of you to ask.'

This surprise invitation from two girls who had not been friends of Tilly's flooded her with emotion. She was on the verge of tears and was finding it hard to control herself. Noticing her distress, they thought-fully suggested finding a corner table, thankfully, not the same one where she had sat with Jacques. There was something special about these two girls. Instantly she felt they were genuinely concerned about her. She didn't feel they were going to judge her. It was such a relief for her to open up to them. Amanda and Immie sat captivated as Tilly opened the floodgates and it all came out, all about how she had been forced to leave the Academy owing to her pregnancy and was now completing her studies by Distance Education. With sadness, she told them how much she missed being a student at the Academy and that playing the flute meant everything to her. She shared the trauma of her mum's illness and how it had left her devas-tated along with how little support she had received from home. Amanda and Immie sat spellbound as she related how she had met Jacques and how she had been swept away in the romance, telling them, 'I felt complete, something I've not felt since Mum died.'

Tilly finished by telling them that she was now living with Jacques' parents. The situation was not ideal. She said, 'How stupid can you get? I had dreams of travelling the world performing at concerts in New York. Now, it looks as though it was just a pipe dream.'

When she left them, after thanking them for being such good listeners, to return to Cynthia and Derek's, she realised she had monopolised the conversation. It was the very first time she'd opened up. The girls had hardly said a thing, just sat and listened. She felt somehow lighter and that a weight had lifted.

When Tilly returned to the cottage, feeling more buoyant than she had for a while, she was surprised to find the lane was filled with cars. Whatever was going off?

'There you are,' shouted Cynthia when she saw Tilly looking apprehensive. 'Come on, we're all waiting for you.' Before Tilly could say a word, Cynthia had grabbed her arm and had firmly led her towards the living room which she was shocked to find was filled with ladies of Cynthia's age. Tilly stood frozen to the spot. She couldn't speak. She didn't know what to say. Someone had strung a paper banner from one side of the window to the other on which was printed in blue and pink lettering BABY SHOWER! Underneath, in smaller letters, Tilly read with horror, All Welcome. To her dismay, she noticed, the dining table was loaded with plates filled with various selections of cakes, many decorated with pink and pale blue icing. There were sandwiches arranged on pink and blue plates. Everyone turned to look at Tilly. Noticing her bewildered expression, one person bravely began to clap. The other guests realising that it might be a good idea to break the tension joined in half-heartedly. Cynthia gently led her to a vacant chair. Noticing Tilly's reluctance, she whispered in her ear, 'Try and look cheerful.'

She was then approached by each lady in turn who gave her a parcel, all of which were wrapped in baby gift wrap in shades of pink and blue. Tilly was in shock. She had never expected this. Part of her wanted to run away as far as she could. Suddenly, she noticed a newcomer had arrived, offering her apologies, for being held up. It was Gillie who on scanning the scene, immediately realised that all was not well and that Tilly wasn't coping. She whispered to Cynthia and quietly went over to Tilly and took her by the arm and led her into the garden. Turning round to face the party guests, she smiled brightly. 'Carry on ladies,' she shouted. 'We'll be back soon.'

In the garden, away from prying eyes, Tilly flung her arms around Gillie and cried and cried. 'How could she?' she repeated clenching her fists with more pressure each time and digging her fingers into Gillie's shoulder.

'Come on, let it all out,' said Gillie gently. 'I warned Cynthia it might be a bit too much for you.'

When Tilly had calmed down, she said, 'I don't know these people and they've all bought gifts for the baby. It's too much. I don't deserve any of it.'

'Accept it with grace. You need clothes, toys, blankets, etc for the baby. Go back in there and pretend to be thrilled and thank them. That's all they want. They are all Cynthia's friends and they want to help. Pretend you are on stage. You can do it. I know you can.'

With Gillie beside her, she returned to the living room, opened the gifts, tiny bootees, knitted jackets, stretch all-in-one suits, blankets and, of course, nappies. It made the baby seem real and it was then that she realised she'd just got to accept it and get on with it.

That night, before she went to bed, she sat next to Cynthia. 'I didn't handle that very well. I'm so sorry. I never expected anything like that. I do appreciate it. Thank you so much.'

'You're welcome love,' was all Cynthia said. 'All I want is for you to have a healthy baby.'

However, uneasiness was causing Tilly some concern. It had been hovering around ever since she had arrived to stay with Cynthia and her husband. It had been growing in intensity over the last few weeks. It was difficult for Tilly to put into words. Cynthia seemed to be obsessed with the baby. All she ever heard was about the baby and it being healthy. It wasn't about her and the baby. On reflection, rarely did Cynthia mention anything about her.

Now, it came to her in a flash. Did Cynthia have other plans for her baby? Who was this baby going to belong to, her or was Cynthia planning on bringing up the baby as her own?

It was at that moment, she decided that the baby would be hers and hers alone. For the first time since she had found out she was pregnant, everything became clear. She was not going to be undermined. The baby would be hers and she would do everything in her power to keep it and prove to everyone that she was capable of being a competent and loving mother.

Chapter 36

Dan thought he'd been patient enough. It was now time to implement his plan. He had been saving hard mainly due to odd jobs like lawn mowing he'd been doing for the neighbours. His Dad was still locked in his depression and had flatly refused to ask for help which Dan found infuriating as he was the one who had to put up with all of his dad's bad moods.

Apart from the new red collar and lead which Dan had previously purchased for when he took Scruffy for his walks, he had returned to the pet shop to buy some essentials. The new dog bed and blanket had been pushed under his bed. The red and blue bowls for food and water were hidden at the back of his wardrobe. The packets of dog food had been placed behind other packets in the pantry.

It was now or never. Pete was dozing in front of the TV. Dan thought this may be a good time to approach his dad when he was half asleep.

'Dad, you know I've been going to the dogs' refuge with Stephie?'

Pete mumbled, which Dan took to mean he'd heard the conversation so far. 'Well, there's a dog there I've been working with. His name is Scruffy. He had a terrible life before he was brought in to the refuge. He used to sit huddled in the corner of the cage and he used to shake whenever anyone came near him. I want to bring him home Dad. I want him to live with me. I'll look after him. You don't have to do anything. OK?'

Dan knew his father had only heard a very small part of his conversation. He repeated the last, 'Will it be OK then Dad?'

'Mm,' his father had grunted.

He didn't care whether his dad had heard his request or had agreed or not. He'd made his mind up. He was going to buy Scruffy.

Chapter 37

IF CYNTHIA WAS AWARE OF A CHANGE IN TILLY, SHE didn't mention it. She noticed the young woman appeared to be more in control of her moods. It was obvious to her that Tilly was determined to complete her studies and was aiming high by the amount of flute playing that was going on which was driving Cynthia around the bend. She had never been a fan of classical music but was having to put up with it daily. Tilly had now cancelled her lessons at the Academy. It was proving too stressful and although Jack Ford was disappointed, he was also relieved.

Tilly had also been taking her pregnancy far more seriously and had been feverishly searching the internet for all the latest research on the correct diet to be followed during pregnancy. Although she had been given a diet sheet when she had first visited the clinic with Gillie, she was now plaguing Cynthia with questions and checking to make sure Cynthia was preparing the correct foods. 'Stop fussing, as if I'd give you anything that would harm the baby! You don't smoke, you don't drink or take drugs and I've never given you anything to cause that, what's its name, begins with an L.'

'Listeria,' Tilly informed her.

'We didn't have to be so faddy when I was pregnant with Jacques. We ate everything we fancied.'

Tilly would respond with all the latest theories and try to explain them to Cynthia.

'My goodness,' she responded, 'you've changed your tune. The next thing you'll be telling me is that you're looking forward to having this baby.'

Cynthia didn't like the expression of disdain on Tilly's face in response to her statement. It made her feel uncomfortable. The two women rarely agreed on anything, especially Cynthia's views on bringing up babies. Things like dipping her finger into the brandy bottle for the baby to lick to help it sleep. That certainly wouldn't be happening. However, Tilly realised that she was on thin ground. She had to keep her views to herself. Cynthia and Derek had offered her a home when she was desperate for somewhere to live and for that she would always be thankful. She tried very hard to fit in and help around the house as much as she was able. Sometimes, she just had to grin and bear it and keep the older woman company when Cynthia's husband was playing bowls at the local sporting club. Sometimes, she caught a look of desperation on Derek's face and saw the sheer relief when he walked towards the car on his time out with the Bowls Team.

Tilly could not fault Cynthia's dedication to the baby's health. She had dutifully taken her to every appointment and had stayed by her side when she had undergone the latest scan. The previous one had been done at 20 weeks which was now a while ago.

The first scan, to which Gillie had attended, had gone by in a blur as Tilly had been too emotional to absorb anything. She certainly hadn't wanted to look at the screen but had turned her head away and had focussed her eyes firmly on a poster on the wall. This hadn't helped at all as the poster featured a healthy, bouncy baby being held by an adoring mother and a besotted father in the background. She remembered her eyes had misted over with tears. This time it had been different.

The radiographer had been very friendly and introduced herself to the two women as Tricia. She had certainly put Tilly at ease. She remembered the cold gel being slathered across her abdomen as she reclined on the examination table. Tricia then used the plastic transducer to glide over her tummy. She explained how she could assess the baby's growth and to make sure the other organs were developing properly. This scan was vitally important; this was when the baby's heart rate would be checked as well as looking at all the major organs. The baby's fingers and toes were counted before Tricia examined the placenta and measured the amniotic fluid levels.

Tricia had told them that she could check on the sex of the baby if Tilly wanted to know. Cynthia had urged her, 'Go on, it'll be more exciting to know, then I can choose the right shade of paint for the nursery, either pale pink or blue.'

However, Tilly had stated in response, 'I'd rather not know. It'll be more exciting to receive a surprise.'

Tilly remembered Cynthia's reaction which had been to huff and puff accompanied by a lot of tutting. Never once did Cynthia ask Tilly to help her choose the paint. She realised it wasn't her house but Cynthia's attitude of taking charge was a red flag warning sign to Tilly. It made the hairs on the back of her neck stand up. Of course, she wasn't insensitive. She could see Cynthia's reasoning behind this. The woman had taken pity on her in her time of need when she had nowhere else to go. She understood this but there was that niggle at the back of her mind. It appeared regularly and deep down in her stomach, Tilly felt a sense of unease. Cynthia had begun to suggest that after Tilly had given birth, she could leave the baby in her capable hands so that Tilly would be free to pursue her musical career. Cynthia had referred to London on more than one occasion.

Back flooded the determination to stand firm and make her point clear. Before she flounced out of the room, she said, 'That's very kind of you but I will not be leaving for London without my baby.'

Chapter 38

DAN SET OUT WITH DETERMINATION WRITTEN ALL OVER his face. He walked purposely down the road towards Stephie's.

'Just about ready,' she said.

As usual, Dan sat in the front seat of the car. Stephie sensed something wasn't right. He appeared very stressed about something. He didn't speak which was most unusual. Stephie noticed he was clutching tightly onto the bag which he used to carry Scruffy's lead and collar. 'Is everything OK?' Stephie dared to ask.

'Fine,' he replied tersely.

'Well, that's good. Have you any news of Tilly?' she asked tentatively as she kept her eyes on the road.

'She seems OK but that woman she's living with is a pain.'

This immediately grabbed Stephie's attention. 'What do you mean? A pain in what way?'

'Well, Tilly mentioned that she thinks she wants to take the baby away from Tilly so she can adopt it.'

'What makes Tilly think that?'

'Well, she wants to make all the decisions.'

'Like what?' asked Stephie with some alarm.

'Well, she wanted to know the sex of the baby when Tilly had the scan a while back, so she could buy the right shade of paint for the nursery. She never asks Tilly for her opinion on anything. Then she told Tilly she would care for the baby whilst Tilly went to study in London.'

'But Tilly would be away for at least two years studying at the Conservatoire. I didn't think she still had a place there. Surely Cynthia is aware of that?'

'She told Tilly she had always wanted another baby and that this will be another chance for her.'

'That's awful! What does Tilly say?'

'That if she went to London the baby would be going with her.'

Stephie didn't have a chance to discuss the matter further as they had driven into the gravel car park of the dogs' refuge and Claudia was waving madly at them in greeting.

'Hi,' she jumped about excitedly. 'Millie has just given birth to nine puppies. Do you want to see them?'

Millie, like all the rest of the inhabitants of the refuge, was a rescue dog who had been left at the locked gates of the refuge a few weeks ago.

'Yes, please,' they both responded. 'Can I ask you something after?' asked Dan with a troubled look on his face.

'Cause you can. You don't need to ask. Spit it out,' she exclaimed in her blunt manner.

'I'll wait until we've seen Millie and the pups,' he responded and turned to walk in the direction of Millie's birthing pen.

Claudia looked at Stephie with raised eyebrows and then back at Dan who was still clutching the bag.

Stephie returned her direct gaze with a shrug of her shoulders.

After they'd all fussed over the pups and cuddled each one. Claudia turned to Dan, 'Well, what's so important? You've not decided to stop coming to the refuge have you?'

'No nothing like that. I've talked to Dad and he says I can buy Scruffy so I'd like to pay for him and take him home today.'

Stephie looked at him in amazement, 'He agreed to you having Scruffy?'

'Yes,' said Dan not looking Stephie in the eye. 'How much is Scruffy? I've brought the money with me, Claudia.'

'I'm not taking the money,' retorted Claudia.

Dan looked as though he was going to burst into tears. 'Why not?'

'I'm not taking any money from you. He's yours as a gift from me to you. You can take him home to keep. If your dad complains, tell him I'm coming round to sort him out.'

They all laughed.

Before the two women had had time to discuss the situation, Dan had raced off to find Scruffy.

When he reappeared with the dog, Scruffy was proudly wearing his red leather collar with the addition of a shiny silver tag engraved with his name, address and telephone number proudly displayed for all to see. Attached to the collar was the shiny red lead Dan had previously purchased. The look on the dog's face said it all. He was standing next to Dan alert, with ears pointing upwards and tail wagging madly. It was as if he knew what had happened and he only had eyes for Dan.

The two women nudged each other. 'I've been waiting for this day for the magic to happen,' they said almost together and laughed again.

'Well, I don't think we'll get much work out of you this afternoon so you'd better take Scruffy for a walk.'

'Be back by 4 o'clock,' said Stephie with a lump in her throat.

Chapter 39

DAN HAD BEEN FULL OF COURAGE WHEN HE HAD FIRST had the idea of owning Scruffy. He had decided that he was going to give the dog a home at all costs. Now, as he left Stephie's house with Scruffy proudly trotting along beside him, he was full of fear. It had started the moment he had begun the homeward journey. Tiny butterflies in his tummy had developed into a huge giant like figure wearing Doc Martens.

Stephie couldn't help but notice Dan's growing agitation as she drove him home. He was hanging on to Scruffy with a vice-like grip. The dog was beginning to look scared.

'Are you OK Dan?' she asked recognising full well that he wasn't.

'I think so,' replied Dan hesitantly.

'You did get your dad's permission to bring Scruffy home with you didn't you?'

'Well, sort of.' He mumbled so quietly that Stephie had to ask him a second time.

'He grunted that it would be OK.'

'Oh, I see,' she kept her eyes firmly on the road and continued, 'but he isn't expecting a dog to arrive home with you is he?'

'It will be a surprise,' replied Dan with a little more courage than he felt. He turned towards Stephie with raise eyebrows and a glint of a smile.

'I'm giving Scruffy a home and if he doesn't like it, too bad,' he said emphatically giving the dog a tight squeeze which made the dog cry out. 'The dog needs me and I need him.'

Stephie looked at Dan and nodded in agreement. 'Well, I'm here if you need me. Fingers crossed. Let me know how it goes.'

When Dan walked into the house, he found his dad still asleep in the armchair. Not unusual for a Saturday afternoon. He silently placed the dog under his arm and crept up the stairs to his room. After placing Scruffy gently on the rug and signalling to him to be quiet, he pulled out the dog bed and blanket from under his bed.

With Scruffy trailing not far behind, Dan dragged the bed down to the kitchen along with the other essentials. It was at this moment that Scruffy heard movement from the lounge room and began to bark. The next moment, Dan's Dad had poked his head around the kitchen door to find out what was going on. The look on his face said it all.

Surprise, quickly followed by disbelief and then followed by anger, Pete yelled, 'What is that dog doing in here?'

Scruffy, sensing the rage emanating from this human that he did not know, let alone trust, began to growl.

Pete, not overly fond of dogs, stepped back. Bravely, Dan said, 'I did mention about having a dog. You must have been asleep and not heard me.' He crossed his fingers behind his back and hoped his father wouldn't notice the white lie.

'Well, I'm waiting,' Pete said leaning against the breakfast bar with his arms folded.

'Well, I've always wanted a dog and Mum said I could have one when I was older. Scruffy needs me. He was left injured by the side of the road. He needs me and I need him, so he's staying,' stated Dan defiantly.

His dad was taken aback by Dan's stance on the matter. For a moment, he was lost for words.

'If you keep the dog, you will have to take care of it, walk it, feed it and keep it out of my hair. Do you understand?' he demanded. Dan nodded his head.

' ... and no taking it upstairs,' he said.

'He's not an IT,' reproached Dan. 'He has a name just like you and me. His name is Scruffy. Come on Scruffy, let's get out of here.'

With a determination, Pete had never witnessed in his son before, Dan, with his shoulders held back and head held high, proudly walked to the front door, down the drive and headed straight for Stephie's house.

'Oh dear!' were her first words. 'Was it that bad?'

'Well, it wasn't good. He says I can keep IT if I look after IT. Scruffy growled at him.'

At that, they both saw the funny side and together they burst into laughter. 'Well, at least you got a reaction!'

'He says, I've got to keep the dog out of his hair. How am I going to do that when I'm at school and he's working at home?'

'Don't worry about that. Bring him down to spend the day with Dizzy. They get on fine. Just look at them.' Both rascals had shot through the dog flap in Stephie's laundry door and were frolicking together on the back lawn and having the time of their doggy lives.

'Come on, it's time for afternoon tea ... and guess what I baked this morning?'

Dan didn't need to guess. Stephie knew what his favourite was ... Date and Orange Cake made from his Mum's recipe. It always brought a smile to Dan's face.

Dan had spent the evening sitting by Scruffy's bed in the kitchen just as he had done at the dogs' refuge. He wanted the dog to feel settled before he climbed the stairs to bed. He could still feel the animosity from his altercation with his dad. It hung in the air like a bad smell. Dan tried to comfort the dog by gently stroking him and talking in a quiet voice. He had sat there until he was so tired he couldn't keep his eyes open any longer and had left a restless Scruffy.

He had just fallen asleep when he was awoken by howls coming from the kitchen. He quickly became fully alert, jumped out of bed and ran down the stairs as quietly as he could. He found Scruffy cowering in his bed. He looked scared. His ears were laid flat against his head and his hind legs were trembling slightly, a definite sign of stress.

'Oh no,' he whispered. 'We can't have that again.' Memories of his first visit to the dogs' home swam before his eyes. The dog, by now was wagging his tail at the sight of his best friend. Dan quickly scooped up the dog in his arms and carried him upstairs.

'I don't care what he says,' he whispered to Scruffy. 'If he won't have you, I'll leave as well. I'll ask Stephie if we can live with her, OK?'

The dog gave him a lick as if in agreement. They snuggled together on Dan's bed and before long, both boy and dog were fast asleep.

Pete had also been disturbed by the noises from the kitchen. Ever since Jo had died, he'd found sleeping difficult. He'd wake up around 2 o'clock on the dot and whatever he did; he couldn't get back to sleep.

Dan's words spoken earlier that day had affected him deeply. Dan had never spoken to him like that before. He'd long forgotten Jo's promise that one day Dan could have a dog. He tried to analyse why he'd become so uptight about a dog. It wasn't too much to ask for. It had never crossed his mind that Dan might be lonely. In fact how long had it been since he'd had a good down to earth chat with his son? He searched his mind. He couldn't find an answer. He'd always left the talking to Jo. Dan and his mum had been close. Sometimes, he'd wondered what they talked about and how the conversations could last for so long.

Now he came to think about it, he'd never been a great talker. It wasn't that he didn't feel things. No, he felt them deeply. It was just that he found difficulty in expressing how he felt.

How did he feel? He didn't know where to begin. There were so many emotions all jammed inside him, weighing him down. It was as though he was an old rag doll who had been stuffed with filling until there was no room for any more. When Jo had first been diagnosed with cancer, it had hit him hard. He felt he had to be strong for her so his emotions had been stored in a special place in his heart. He had never discussed the fear he'd felt when he thought he might lose his wife. He couldn't talk to Jo about losing her. She'd always been so positive. She was adamant she was going to conquer the disease. When the cancer returned, she had remained positive. However, Pete couldn't see it through her eyes. He had hidden his emotions. The storage space in his heart just got heavier.

Since her death, that weight had just become impossible to shift. To get up in the morning, shower and prepare himself for work was all he was capable of. Work helped him as concentrating on his clients took his mind off his problems.

It would be true to say that Pete was not in a good place mentally. When he'd received the news about

Tilly, he'd flown into an immediate rage. He couldn't take it in. She'd always been his perfect princess. He had worshipped her from the day she'd been born. Now that he thought about it, had he ever told her how much she meant to him and that he loved her? To receive the news that his bright, talented, seventeen-year-old daughter, who had the world at her feet, had been intimate with a guy and was pregnant was the last thing he ever expected to hear.

Instead of talking to his daughter and finding out her side of things, he'd hit the roof. His immediate reaction was one of horror quickly followed by disgust and shame. Disowning his daughter didn't mean he didn't love or care for her, it was his way of saying he couldn't take anymore.

His thoughts drifted back to the funeral and Stephie. He had to admit she'd been a tower of strength to Jo. When he'd seen her in the kitchen, his mind had flipped. He didn't want another woman in his kitchen. He only wanted Jo and so his reaction had been to lash out. Now there was the dog. Was Dan so bereft he'd felt compounded to bond with a stray dog?

What a mess everything was in! What a mess he was in!

When Pete had heard the dog howling, he had stayed quietly in his room. His door was slightly ajar and he was surprised to hear Dan whispering in deep conversation with the dog. He tried to remember the last time he and Dan had discussed anything at length. Since Jo had died, he'd closed his heart to everyone. It was easier not to become close to other people. His daughter had let him down. He couldn't cope with anymore hurt and pain.

After a couple of minutes, he heard Dan walk up the stairs. It was obvious he had the dog with him as he was still whispering to him. Pete picked up on, 'Come on Scruffy, you're staying with me whatever he says.'

With these words going round and round in his head, he knew he wouldn't sleep. After tossing and turning in a crumpled bed for over half an hour, Pete got up, stepped across the corridor to Dan's bedroom and peered around the half-open door. With the light of the moon shining through a gap in the curtains, he could see his son and the dog, Scruffy, huddled together, fast asleep breathing in perfect harmony. He returned to his room, his brain in turmoil, his body in shock. For the first time since his wife's death, he collapsed onto his bed in the foetal position and broke into gut-wrenching sobs.

Dan awoke after a very troubled night. He wasn't sure what kind of reception he was going to receive when he went downstairs. It was obvious that Scruffy had spent most of the night upstairs asleep on his bed.

Upon entering the kitchen, he noticed that his dad appeared dishevelled and bleary-eyed. 'Morning son,' he volunteered.

'Morning Dad,' he responded, unsure of what the next move might be. Normally smartly attired in slate grey pants, white shirt and tie, this morning, Pete was still wearing crumpled pyjamas and his old dressing gown. Dan was amazed when his dad tentatively bent at the knees and reached out towards Scruffy, gently patting the astonished dog on the head. 'Hi Scruffy, welcome.'

Well, this certainly was unexpected. Scruffy was quite perceptive. With Dan by his side, he stood and stared intently at Pete. It was as though the dog was trying to read the thoughts of this human who seemed so troubled.

'I'm not going to do any work this morning,' he said to a surprised Dan. 'I've got some things to sort out.'

'Are you OK Dad?' asked Dan apprehensively.

''Not too good at the moment but it'll all work out, don't worry.'

Chapter 40

DAN HAD A HABIT OF BOUNCING INTO STEPHIE'S HOUSE. This morning he was accompanied by Scruffy who looked decidedly pleased with himself. His tail was wagging madly and he was wearing a new tartan coat, a surprise gift from Dan purchased earlier that morning as the weather was still quite chilly.

Of course, she'd expected Dan to be buoyed up with the arrival of Scruffy but there was a distinct change in the air. There was a lightness in the atmosphere. She couldn't pinpoint it but she sensed Dan was about to announce something really important. Stephie looked at him expectantly, 'You look chuffed this morning,' she said. 'Come on spill the beans.'

It's quite a long story so you might want to sit down, 'said Dan.

'That sounds ominous. It isn't bad news about Tilly is it?'

'No, no, nothing like that,' Dan assured her.

Dan, not wanting to keep Stephie in suspense, related the events of the previous night. He would never let his dad know that he'd heard the choked sobs coming from his room across the hallway.

'At last! I wondered how long it would take before your dad collapsed and crumbled. He's been holding his emotions inside like a tightly coiled spring. I knew it would unwind one day. We've got Scruffy to thank for that. He's a little miracle worker.'

Stephie knelt on the carpet and flung her arms around the dog's neck. 'You are a cutie,' she said before giving Scruffy a big kiss on his forehead. 'You deserve a treat.' With that, she disappeared into the kitchen and found Dizzy's tin of Doggie chocolate treats. Dizzy, not wanting to be left out, pushed herself in front of Scruffy and with front paws in the air was begging with all her might.

Both Stephie and Dan burst out laughing. 'Look at the pair of them! We'll have to make sure Scruffy doesn't get as spoilt as Princess Dizzy.' After both dogs had received a treat they were sent off into the back garden.

'I know it's a bit early, but I think that news calls for a celebration. How about we take the dogs to the park and afterwards call in at the French Patisserie. I'll treat you to whatever you like.'

Knowing how far Dan's appetite could stretch, Stephie wondered if she'd said the right thing. Dan reading her mind, joked, 'Well, I'll start with one of their French salad baguettes, followed by a French Éclair. I think I'd still have room for a slice of Apricot and Raspberry Country Tart or should I have a slice of Chocolate Tart with Gold Leaf?'

'Hey! Hold it there. I think that may be enough. You know how sweet their desserts are. I don't want to be responsible for you spending the whole evening in the bathroom.'

'Wow! Well, Í can't refuse an offer like that,' said Dan with a great grin written from one side of his face to the other.

Stephie couldn't help but feel relief. It was such a long time since she'd seen Dan in such a relaxed mood. It was great to see him with a smile from ear to ear.

Before they left for the park, Stephie said, 'It's really good news about your dad but you know it's not going to be easy for him don't you?'

'It can't be much worse than it's been recently.'

'That's true,' agreed Stephie.

~

It had been an eventful day in more ways than one. Stephie sat in her favourite armchair overlooking her back garden. That evening she was not interested in watching the TV or reading or listening to music. She had far too much on her mind.

Pete had unexpectedly called round late in the afternoon. He was the last person Stephie was expecting to see. She thought back to the moment she had opened the front door. Shocked beyond words, she had kept the front door half open grabbing onto the doorknob to steady herself. Noticing her stunned expression and sensing her reluctance to see him, Pete was about to turn and retreat down the path to the gate.

'No, no, don't go,' she'd managed to stammer.

'Are you sure?' Pete replied with difficulty. 'I don't want to be a nuisance. I haven't come to cause trouble.'

Stephie quickly regained her composure. 'Well, I must admit that this is a surprise,' she managed to mumble. 'You'd better come in.'

Pete was clutching a huge bouquet. 'I've come to apologise for my disgraceful behaviour. If I'm not welcome, I'll go. I'll understand after all that's happened.' Nervously, he continued, 'I hope you can forgive me.'

What she didn't anticipate was Pete's meltdown. Upon entering the house he suddenly burst into heavy sobs interspersed by gulps for air. She directed him to a chair, gently took the flowers from him and laid them on the nearby table. She placed a box of tissues on the chair arm, sat down opposite him and waited in silence until this sudden outburst of grief had subsided.

When he had recovered enough to speak, he hesitantly said in such a quiet voice that Stephie had to strain to hear him, 'I don't know what to say.' Still clutching the sopping wet tissues, he was finding it difficult to look at her.

She responded, 'I'm relieved you are, at last, letting out your grief. You've bottled it up for so long. The bubble was bound to burst sometime. It's better to let it out with friends.'

'Do you mean that?' he whispered.

'Of course, I've been a friend of yours from the moment Jo introduced us. It's just that circumstances have interrupted our friendship for a while.'

'I've come to tell you that I've been to see my GP this morning. He's arranging for me to see a grief counsellor and has prescribed medication temporarily to help me cope. It's not going to be easy but I can't continue as I am at the moment.' Twiddling his fingers he continued, 'I've not been fair to the children, especially Tilly. I feel dreadful about the way I've treated her. The latest news about her pregnancy, you know, has been such a shock. I haven't handled it well. She was my princess, you know? I was always so proud of her. She was a replica of her mother, talented, so talented with the world at her feet. I couldn't take the news in of her ... you know what I mean? Not my Tilly. Everything just fell apart in a big way. I don't suppose you know how she is?'

'Yes, it's been a hard time for all of us. I know I was shocked to hear the news about the baby. It doesn't seem real does it?' She paused and when there was no answer, she offered, 'I haven't the latest news from Tilly but I'll try to find out. Do you have a message for her?'

'Tell her,' he floundered, 'tell her I'm so sorry and ... that I love her.' With that, he burst out into uncontrollable sobs again.

After he'd left, Stephie couldn't stop thinking about the events of the day. She felt quite drained and didn't think she'd sleep well that night. However, she did what she always did before she slipped between the sheets and that was to pray.

It had been a peculiar day. She had a lot to be grateful for on this particular evening. For some reason, it was Scruffy who came into her mind first, that adorable scrap of fur playing such an important role in Dan's life. In her prayers, she thanked Claudia for rescuing Scruffy and giving him a second chance.

Dan came next on this list. He still needed so much guidance after losing his mum. Slowly he was getting there but there were so many other complications in his life. Then it was Pete's turn. She included a special prayer of thanks that, with help and guidance, he could begin to work through the grieving process.

When she came to Tilly, she didn't know where to begin. How she missed her and wished she could go and scoop her up and bring her home to be reunited with her family where she belonged. It wasn't right that she was so far away from home living with strangers.

Lastly, she prayed for guidance, which she so desperately needed, and for strength to help all these people who she loved so deeply. She made a promise that she would find out how Tilly was faring. She would do it the very next morning.

Chapter 41

Tilly was now seven months pregnant. She could no longer hide her pregnancy under billowing dresses. It was plain for all to see. She should have been relaxing and preparing herself mentally as well as physically for the birth. Everything was set in place. A hospital room had been booked and Cynthia was adamant she was going to be Tilly's birthing partner. What could go wrong?

However, the two women were poles apart. Cynthia was fussy and had a tendency to be overpowering and it was this trait that was concerning Tilly who, on the other hand, was serious and kept to the point. Yes, Cynthia had willingly ferried her backward and forwards to her appointments and had arranged for a social worker to give extra support as well as a visit to Centrelink where she found she could access extra payments for her and the baby. She was so involved that anyone would have thought Cynthia was the expectant Mum.

However, it was Cynthia's overzealous behaviour that persisted in bugging her. The older woman appeared very uptight. She had not taken it at all well that Tilly had decided to wait until the birth to find out the sex of the baby. She repeatedly admonished Tilly for all the extra work this was causing her. Tilly failed to understand the reason behind these thought patterns.

As soon as Derek left for work, his wife was to be found huddled over the laptop at the kitchen table searching online for nursery room equipment, clothing, toiletries, baby baths, toys, etc. Instead of relaxing Tilly had spent ages trying to analyse what was going on. Something wasn't right. She was most concerned that Cynthia had ulterior motives. Instead of feeling excited and safe, this behaviour was eating at every fibre in her body.

It was when the deliveries began that things started to get out of hand. At first, it was small packages that could easily be stored away before Derek arrived home. However, this had graduated to parcels and boxes that were being delivered by the Post Office delivery vans and from DHL.

On this particular day, when Derek arrived home from work, he couldn't believe his eyes. Unopened boxes were lined up in the hall. On closer inspection, there appeared to be two of everything. The whole hall was cluttered to the extent, he couldn't reach the kitchen. 'What's going on here?' he shouted. 'Are we starting a business?'

From upstairs, Cynthia replied, 'It's all her fault.'

'What do you mean her fault?' asked Derek as the accusing finger was being pointed at a very embarrassed Tilly.

'She refused to tell me whether the baby is a boy or a girl, so I've had to order two of each item, one in pink, the other in blue.'

'Well, you could have ordered just one in white until you found out,' admonished her husband. 'What are we going to do with all the extra stuff we don't need? We can't afford to buy two of everything.'

Tilly was by now on the verge of tears. 'I didn't ask for any of this,' she said as she pointed to everything. 'I'll help you to pay. I've got some savings.'

'If it had been up to you,' Cynthia shouted, 'the baby would have been sleeping in a cardboard box.'

'Now, now, no need to speak to Tilly like that,' replied Derek sternly. 'Don't worry Tilly. We'll sort it out,' he said as he shook his head in disbelief.

Derek realised that all of this was Cynthia's doing. He knew his wife, and he was becoming increasingly concerned about her mental health.

As Tilly had mentioned to Dan during one of their infrequent calls, Cynthia had been busy decorating the upstairs spare room. Motifs of butterflies were ready to be assembled onto the freshly painted pink walls.

'Of course, I may have to repaint all of this in blue!' she shouted at Derek as he clambered over the boxes to reach the newly painted nursery.

'I didn't ask for pink paint,' Tilly remonstrated. 'I would be quite happy with white.'

'We can't have white! It's got to be pink or blue, you stupid girl!' she shouted in exasperation.

'Come on downstairs and let's have a cuppa,' Derek suggested to calm the situation down. However, it did the opposite, 'Soon as I've finished placing these butterflies on the wall,' she shouted, followed by, 'and when she's had this baby, whatever it is, she can leave me in peace and go off and do her own thing.'

By now Derek was beginning to see where all of this was leading. 'I think you need to go and lie down,' he suggested to his wife as he gently removed a butterfly motif from Cynthia's tightly clenched fist. Running his hands through the thin strands of hair that were left covering his head, he put his free arm around her shoulders and led his distraught wife into their room.

Tilly was getting desperate. The baby was kicking like mad and her heart was beating in unison. The recent conversation she had had with Dan when he'd told her about Scruffy flashed before her eyes. 'Oh, Til! I wish you'd come home. I miss you so much. You and the baby would love Scruffy.'

'Oh, how I wish it were possible but you know it isn't Dan. I miss you too,' she'd replied regretfully before bursting into tears.

Chapter 42

Tilly kept herself busy. She had exams to prepare for. Even though she was no longer a student at St C's, Gillie had managed to arrange for Tilly to sit her exams at an independent centre in the city. She continued to practice the flute. It was a welcome release from all of her problems, the main one being Cynthia. Tilly was becoming unnerved. The fact that the older woman was concerned for Tilly's health was commendable. She could only admire the effort she was putting into preparing for the baby's arrival. What was concerning Tilly more than anything was the constant references to after the baby was born.

'Not long now before you'll be free,' was the latest comment.

'What do you mean, I'll be free?' enquired Tilly with trepidation.

'What I meant was, you'll be free to follow your dreams, travel overseas and attend that Conservatoire you're always going on about.'

'I originally had provisional places at the

Conservatoire de Paris and the Royal School of Music in London. I'd chosen London; however, it's a bit too late for that now. I've had to withdraw my application. How would I have managed to study there with a baby to look after?' asked Tilly who was standing with arms protectively wrapped around her belly.

'Well, I've been thinking about that. As you don't really want this baby, you could leave it here with me. I could look after it for you.'

With indignation, Tilly rose to her full height, looked Cynthia straight in the eye and responded, 'The baby is mine and I do want it and I'm going to be the one who looks after it, not you!'

'Well, that's a change in attitude,' Cynthia retorted. 'After all, I've done for you, kept you off the streets, fed and cared for you. There's no pleasing some people. You're nothing but a little ...'

Unbeknown to Cynthia, and before she could finish her sentence, Derek had appeared and had witnessed the last part of the conversation. 'That's enough Cynthia. Tilly has become part of our family. Of course, she's not planning on leaving the baby here with us, are you love?'

Tilly felt like screaming. What was going on? When she'd first gone to live with Cynthia and Derek it had been difficult. She didn't know this couple. Cynthia had made her welcome. However, the more Tilly thought about it, she realised that Cynthia had altered. All she was concerned about was the baby, not her.

Did she really think she could take her baby as if it were her own? She knew Cynthia had wanted more babies when she was young. Surely she didn't think she could adopt her baby and that she would walk out the door to fly off to far-flung places like London and never return?

She could feel the tension rising inside her body. She wanted to shout, stamp her feet and scream. Any minute now and she would explode. She was aware that her heartbeat was racing. She could feel the beats banging in her chest. She was shaking from head to foot and finding it difficult to breathe. Any second now a panic attack would begin. She felt her baby kicking madly in response to this trauma. Her reaction was to cling onto the back of the settee whilst she tried to fight the wild panting that was overtaking her body. Before the ground swallowed her up, she felt Derek's strong arms around her shoulders. She found herself being led to the settee. 'Come on love,' he said gently, 'deep breaths. Count with me, one, two,' and so he continued talking her through it gently.

When Tilly's breathing became more controlled, she noticed Cynthia was no longer in the room. She could hear loud sobs coming from the garden. 'Don't worry about her,' Derek muttered shaking his head. 'She'll get over it. No one's going to take your baby away from you.'

Just then, her mobile phone rang. 'Are you going to answer that or shall I?' Derek asked. With Tilly still not fully in control, she nodded for him to take charge. The relief washed over him when he realised who was speaking and he passed the phone over to her, mouthing, 'Stephie.'

The relief was overwhelming.

'Hi, it's Stephie. I haven't heard from you for a while and wondered how you're doing?'

Stephie didn't expect her call to have such a profound impact. All she could hear was heart-wrenching sobs. She immediately went into panic mode. What an earth was the matter? 'Tilly, I'm here. Are you OK? What's the matter? Tell me what's wrong? Is it the baby?'

'Oh Stephie, I need you. Please come,' replied a voice so raw with emotion that Stephie didn't recognise it.

A male voice appeared to step in and take over. 'Hi, it's Derek, Cynthia's husband. To answer your question, the baby is OK. Tilly isn't so good. I'd say she needs her family.'

Stephie introduced herself. Derek replied, 'I know who you are. I've heard a lot about you from Tilly.'

'Do you mind if I visit?' asked Stephie tentatively. She was desperate with worry but didn't want to sound too keen in case the answer was in the negative.

In that split second, the situation had reached a climax. Stephie was horrified. There was a commotion and she could hear raised voices in the background. Tilly was screaming, 'It's my baby. It's not yours to take.'

Cynthia responded with, 'You're not fit to be a mother! You don't want this baby. This is the baby I lost. It's mine.'

It didn't need any explanation as to what was happening. The picture was clear. She decided she was going to rescue Tilly before there was any harm done. She didn't need approval. She didn't care whether Cynthia and Derek wanted her to visit. She was going, like it or not. She had never moved so fast. A weekend bag was packed with haste. She hurriedly texted Dan to tell him what was happening and asked him to call in to look after Dizzy.

Before she left she texted Tilly with the message, 'I'm on my way. Stay strong.'

Chapter 43

THANKFULLY, DEREK WAS PLACID. HE APPROACHED LIFE calmly and he appeared capable of handling any stresses that were thrown in his direction. He was also astute. Why, oh why had it not entered his head until this moment? His thoughts led him back to the early years of his married life. Cynthia had been bereft when she had lost the babies. He had struggled too but Cynthia had been devastated. How could he have forgotten how she'd had to take anti-depressants for a while? He remembered he'd encouraged her to visit a grief counsellor and although it had helped, she hadn't improved until Jacques had arrived.

Jacques had been the answer to her prayers. She had idolised him to the point where on occasions, Derek had felt ignored and unimportant. They had both taken their son's recent disappearance badly. However, the mind works in mysterious ways and he'd not realised how Cynthia's attitude towards Tilly had altered. At first, she'd shown the girl love and concern but now that he came to think of it, all the attention had been transferred to the baby. He thought of the baby shower which had been arranged without Tilly's knowledge. Then there'd been all of the purchases for the baby and the decorating of the nursery without any consultation with Tilly. Yes, Cynthia had shown great concern about the girl's health but there had been little consideration as to the girl's welfare, not towards the end at any rate. Now, with all these references to Tilly departing to go overseas, it all made perfect sense. His wife was heading for a major breakdown and needed help and so did Tilly.

Chapter 44

Tilly couldn't believe the speed in which events happened. It was all a blur. The emergency doctor had arrived and had assessed Cynthia and had made arrangements for her to be taken into hospital. Much later that evening, after a long drive, Stephie had arrived insisting that Tilly pack her belongings and return with her where she belonged.

When poor Derek arrived back from the hospital, he was in a state of shock. He had experienced a torrid time with Cynthia in the emergency department. She had been completely beside herself, ranting and raving to everyone nearby that her baby was being taken away from her by the snip of a girl who wasn't suitable to be a mother. He had left her in the capable hands of the doctors who had given her strong sedatives. This woman was not the Cynthia he knew and loved. 'God, what a mess! Please help us all,' he whispered whilst desperately hoping someone was listening.

Derek was such a kind man. On his arrival home, he wasn't surprised to see the packed cases lined up by the front door. He didn't want to see Tilly leave as he had become fond of her and was looking forward to playing a part in the life of his grandchild. Deep down he realised it was for the best.

He found Stephie perched on the edge of the settee in the sitting room. 'Would you like a cup of tea before you leave?' he asked.

Stephie replied with a warm smile, 'You sit down. You look all in. I'll go to make a pot of tea. Tilly will be downstairs when she's finished sorting some things out.'

Derek was grateful for Stephie's consideration. He did feel terrible as if all his get up and go had suddenly blown out of the window and left him empty. When she returned with the tea, he said, 'I'm not proud of my son, you know. To be honest, his behaviour has appalled me. Tilly's a lovely girl but they weren't suited. Jacques has been spoilt all of his life. He needs to take responsibility for his actions but somehow, I've got a feeling that won't happen. He doesn't appear to have a conscience. That's an awful thing for a man to say about his son but it's true.'

Stephie nodded her head in sympathy. She didn't know what to say. The situation was a mess.

After a sip of his tea, Derek continued, 'My focus now is to support Cynth. She'll need a lot of care when she comes home, and honestly, having Tilly here wouldn't help.'

Again Stephie nodded. Tilly had appeared and she

turned to the girl saying, 'Well, have you got everything?'

She noticed Tilly was again on the verge of tears so, she quickly said, 'Well, I think we should make a move. If we go now, the roads will be quiet and we should be home not long after midnight.'

Tilly stood hesitantly, walked towards Derek and tentatively hugged him. 'Thank you for looking after me. I feel terrible that it's all ended like this.'

'Look after yourself love. Please keep in touch and let us know how things go. Perhaps when things are back to normal and Cynthia is feeling better, you'll visit with the baby.'

Tilly nodded. At that moment all that was on her mind was to get as far away from the house as possible.

Chapter 45

IT WAS WITH MIXED EMOTIONS AND A CERTAIN AMOUNT of fear that Tilly entered Stephie's house early the next morning. She had been assured on the journey that she would have a home with Stephie for as long as she needed. Stephie reminded Tilly that she had promised her mum that she would be there for both her and Dan and that she was now able to carry out that promise.

'But what about Dad?' Tilly asked with concern written all over her face.

'Don't worry. Leave me to deal with him. I'll go and explain it all to him in the morning. He's attending grief counselling now and he's trying to come to terms with all that's happened. Give him time. All you have to worry about is having a healthy baby and looking after your own needs. There's no pressure on you to do anything else. It will all sort itself out.'

'But what about my exams?' asked Tilly. 'I've been revising like mad and Gillie has made arrangements for me to sit the exams. I'll never be able to continue my flute studies if I don't.' Tilly was becoming hysterical.

She had begun to tremble and Stephie was concerned.

'It's late and you need to go to bed. How about a milky drink? It'll help you to sleep.'

When Tilly nodded Stephie continued, 'I realise everything seems to be in a mess at the moment, and to tell you to stop worrying is stupid. If I was in your position, I'd be worried too. I'll contact Gillie in the morning to explain and I think it would be a good idea to arrange for you to have a check-up. We can make decisions after that. Come on sleepyhead, I'll take you up to your room.'

Chapter 46

Tilly was led up to Stephie's guest room which was furnished very simply. The room was small. The walls had been painted in off-white. A crisp white duvet and matching pillows decorated the bed. Soft white curtains in a sheer floaty fabric hung at the window and a pale grey pull-down blind had been added to shade the room from the heat of the sun and to give privacy at night. Stephie had added a red-framed full-length mirror and prints on the walls. The atmosphere was one of peace and serenity which is just what Tilly needed. Tilly thought it was just perfect. For the first time in months, she felt herself beginning to relax. She whispered, 'I'm home,' and immediately was swept away into a dream world of love and security.

When she awoke the next morning, she couldn't work out where she was. Then, it all came flooding back, the events of the previous day. She shuddered and tried to block out the thoughts swirling around in her head. Words that had been spoken in haste, which had the power to destroy another person, but then she reminded herself that Cynthia was unwell and didn't mean what she'd said. She looked around the room again and whispered, 'Oh Stephie, thank you for rescuing me.'

When she arrived in the kitchen, she found a note propped up against a cereal packet. Tilly read, 'Make yourself at home. I've gone to chat with your dad. Everything's in the fridge, milk, butter, bread, marmalade. Coffee, tea, whatever else you want is in the cupboard. Don't worry, see you soon.'

Tilly's decision making about breakfast was suddenly interrupted when the door was flung open and in walked Dan followed by Scruffy. He flung his arms around Tilly's neck and as soon as Scruffy realised that his master liked the new girl, he was wagging his tail and jumping up and down in welcome. Dizzy, who had been in the back garden suddenly emerged as soon as she realised that her two best friends, Dan and Scruffy had arrived and she joined in the welcome greetings.

When Stephie appeared, she was overjoyed to see that the brother and sister were enjoying a heartfelt hug. It was great to see that the reunion, which with the help of the dogs, had brought a welcome smile to Tilly's face. 'It'll all be fine,' she said to herself. 'We'll weather the storm together.'

The conversation with Pete had gone well considering his previous antagonism towards his daughter.

Unbeknown to Stephie and Dan, he had discussed the pregnancy at length and how it was affecting him with his counsellor. She had tried to put the whole episode into perceptive. It would take a while before he felt comfortable with his daughter's situation but he had all the time in the world to work on it. Deep down, although he wasn't prepared to admit it, he was looking forward to becoming a grandparent.

Pete asked Stephie to give his daughter a message, 'Ask her if I can call around and tell her I love her.'

Later that morning whilst Tilly was taking the time to unpack and make herself feel more at home, Stephie had disappeared into her study for an in-depth conversation with Gillie on Skype. Stephie was keen to sound out the views of another woman who had Tilly's best interest at heart.

They both agreed that it was vital for Tilly to have time off before the birth, both for her sake as much as that of the baby. She had experienced enough traumatic episodes to last her a lifetime. The latest episode at Cynthia's had done nothing to calm down Tilly's already jangled nerves. She desperately needed time to process all that had happened since the death of her mum. She needed time to grieve with support from those around her and time to prepare herself both physically and mentally for becoming a Mum. Both women agreed that exams should be the last thing on her mind. Now Stephie had to pass on this information to Tilly.

As Stephie anticipated, the news was not taken at all well. Tilly became extremely agitated and was adamant that she was capable of sitting the exams. 'I have to sit for the exams! I've done all the preparation. I'll never be able to study flute without my results!'

Stephie realising she had to take control of the situation suggested she make a coffee and they go out to sit in the garden. When they were seated, Stephie said, 'First of all, I think it would be a good idea if I made an appointment for you to see a doctor, just to check out everything's fine. What do you think?'

Tilly nodded but Stephie could sense reluctance. 'We do need to see if this baby is alright, don't you think?' Stephie didn't share her thoughts, but deep down she was more concerned about Tilly than she was about the baby.

'Just as long as it's a female doctor,' she replied with resignation.

Stephie was lucky to get a cancellation appointment at the local surgery with a young female doctor, who asked her patients to refer to her as Dr Jane. It just so happened that Jane was the owner of a giant black poodle called Sophie and was also a member of Stephie's dog walking group. Stephie and Jane had struck up a strong friendship and Stephie had mentioned Tilly on more than one occasion whilst strolling around the dog park. As Tilly wasn't a patient of the doctor's at the time of the chats, patient confidentiality didn't apply. However, there would be no more references to Tilly's situation outside of the consulting room.

'How are you feeling?' she asked Tilly. 'Your blood pressure is a little too high for my liking. I need you to pop out to the bathroom as I need a urine sample.' On passing a small plastic jar to Tilly, she said, 'I'll see you in a minute, third door on the left.'

When Tilly had left the room, the Dr looked at Stephie. Physically, she's underweight for a start. I'm concerned about her blood pressure. With a reading that high, there's a chance of her developing pre-eclampsia. Let's just hope it's to do with her stress levels. Mentally, I can tell just by looking at her and noticing her reactions that she's not in good shape. Has she booked a bed at the maternity hospital?'

Stephie was taken aback by the reaction of the doctor. 'Well no, not yet. She only arrived last night. She had it all arranged but with the sudden move here last night, nothing's been done.'

Tilly had by now arrived back in the surgery and the doctor was testing the protein levels in her urine. She looked directly at Tilly and said kindly, 'I don't want to worry you but because your blood pressure is so high, I want you to go home and have total bed rest.'

Stephie felt things couldn't get much worse.

Tilly, with an expression of horror written across her face, blurted out, 'But what about my exams? I've got to take them!'

Dr Jane responded, 'I'm so sorry. I know how important those exams are to you but listen to me, you are at risk of developing pre-eclampsia or even eclampsia. Without monitoring and rest, you could lose the baby and put your own life at risk. I know it's hard to take but we have to face the facts. I want you to go home and rest. Let Stephie take care of you.' She looked at Stephie and asked, 'Do you, by any chance have a blood pressure monitor at home?'

When Stephie nodded, she continued, 'That's great! I'd like you to check Tilly's blood pressure at regular intervals throughout the day.' She continued to give Stephie the details and said she wanted to see Tilly again later in the week. She finished the consultation with, 'If there's any change for the worst, ring for an ambulance.'

Stephie nodded.

'Is it as bad as that?' asked a very troubled Tilly.

'It's not too bad at the moment. Let's try and see if we can lower that blood pressure by resting. All the stress you've been under hasn't helped. Promise me, you'll do as Stephie tells you.'

Tilly, biting her bottom lip, nodded. 'I promise,' she replied reluctantly.

Chapter 47

IT WAS A VERY DEJECTED TILLY WHO ARRIVED BACK AT Stephie's. Even Dizzy's joyful welcome failed to bring a smile to her face. Stephie realised she had a hard task ahead of her. She had taken Jane's advice seriously and had no intention of letting anything happen to Tilly or the baby. 'Come on, swivel round and put your legs up on the end of the settee. What you need is plenty of rest and for you to stop worrying. It will help lower your blood pressure. First of all, I'm going to feed you up.' With that, she disappeared into the kitchen and returned with a tray of delicious fruit snacks, a bowl of yoghurt, a slice of cake and a glass of milk.

Stephie had some news for Tilly which she hoped would be a start in lifting her spirits. As the girl was so despondent she said, 'I wasn't going to mention anything until I was more certain, but you look so downhearted, and I think you need something to cheer you up.'

Tilly was attempting to eat the fruit. It all seemed to be too much of an effort. She didn't appear interested in anything. That was until Stephie said, 'What if I told you I think I may have found a plan that would mean you could still study flute without taking those exams?'

Tilly's eyes brightened and she started to show some interest. 'It's not possible. What do you mean?'

'Well, nothing's certain, and don't raise your hopes too high, but I think you stand a good chance.'

'A good chance at what? Please tell me. Don't keep me in suspense.'

'Well, I found a post on Facebook about a young male dancer who had emigrated from overseas and was amazingly talented. He just didn't have the prerequisites to get into a ballet school or University to study dance. However, and this is where it gets really exciting, he attended a special college for performers and after three years of study, he graduated with a degree. He's now a leading dancer in London. Isn't that amazing?'

Tilly responded with, 'Well that's great for him but how does it help me?'

'Wait for it! The college is here in Sydney ... and they teach flute! Just something for you to consider,' Stephie said with a great big smile written across her face.

Two days later, it was time for Tilly to return to the doctor who noticed the change in Tilly immediately, 'What have you been doing?' she asked. 'Your blood pressure has dropped and you're looking much happier. Keep it up, then we'll have a healthy Mum and baby.'

Tilly responded with, 'It's all down to Stephie.'

The time for the birth was getting closer and Tilly had settled into a routine. She had booked into the local hospital, been examined by an obstetrician and had met the midwife. She was delighted when Stephie had agreed to be her birthing partner. Together, they attended all the necessary appointments and had joined a pregnancy yoga class for Mums and their birth partners.

The nursery had been decorated and this time, Tilly had chosen the colour scheme and furnishings. Dan and his dad were frequent visitors to Stephie's house. They were always accompanied by Scruffy, who with Dizzy had the knack of cheering everyone up with their wild doggy antics. Pete was slowly resolving his problems and was becoming closer to his daughter.

Stephie had asked Tilly if she would like her to make inquiries at the college on her behalf. The next thing Tilly knew about it was a large A4 envelope arriving addressed to her. It offered her an open interview and an audition. The place was not dependant on her final year exams.

The news certainly gave Tilly something to focus on during the last weeks of her pregnancy. Stephie was so delighted to see her practising the piece she had chosen for the audition. It was *Morceau de Concours* by the French composer Gabriel Fauré.

Acknowledging her talent at the audition and taking into consideration her previous academic results from St C's, the college had agreed wholeheartedly to offer her a place. They were quite happy for the place to be held for her until she felt ready to start on her studies again.

Tilly realised how fortunate she had been. The ending could have been quite different. There was such a lot to look forward to. She would be forever grateful for Stephie's love and support. The pregnancy felt as though it had gone on for years not just nine months! All she needed now was time to find herself again, time to bond with her baby and time to spend with those she truly loved. She was surrounded by love and support and the future looked bright. What more could she ask for?

However, there was one more surprise for Tilly. Stephie had shared the news with Tilly that she had decided to take early retirement. She wanted to honour her promise to Jo that she would be there for her children. Perhaps things had not worked out how Jo would have hoped. However, Stephie was adamant that Tilly and the baby could stay with her as long as they needed a home. Secretly, she, like Pete, was excited about the baby. For Stephie, it was a dream come true. She had never met the man of her dreams and she was long over the age of having a child herself. To be an honorary grandma was a special gift.

Epilogue

6 Years Later

WHEN TILLY LOOKED BACK ON HER YOUNG LIFE, SHE had as the saying goes, 'been to hell and back again.' If it had not been for Stephie, who had read a post on Facebook, she doubted she would be standing on this stage tonight making her debut as a solo flautist accompanied by the state's symphony orchestra and playing in front of a packed audience.

The birth of Stephanie-Jo had meant that Tilly had been forced to grow up fast. She was responsible for the life of another human being. Even so, Stephie had encouraged her to go out and have fun, telling her she was only young once.

Stephie had been amazing. Not only had she willingly taken early retirement to support Tilly and the baby, but she was also instrumental in assisting Pete with his journey through the grieving process. She had proved to be a superb substitute mum and best friend to Dan. She was a truly remarkable woman who had carried out her promise, at long last, to her best friend Jo.

Proudly, Tilly stood centre stage. The applause was overwhelming. She clasped tightly onto the huge bouquet she had been presented with, raised her head and smiled a smile that spoke volumes.

The auditorium was dark. However, she was familiar with the layout of the seating in the concert hall. She could just see the outlines of the most important people in her life. It made her heart sing almost to bursting to see them all there together. She could pick out her Dad and Stephie, who were now the best of friends. Next to them were Dan and his new girlfriend. A small girl of around 6 years of age with huge hazel eyes looked up towards her mum with pride and gave a gentle wave. By her side sat a new member who had joined the family group, a few months ago, Tilly's partner, Tim, a young and talented violinist as well as being an aspiring conductor. It was a joy that he had accepted Stephanie-Jo as his daughter. He was applauding loudly and when he caught her eye, he blew her a kiss. Next to him sat Cynthia and Derek. Cynthia had recovered from her illness and was now boasting to everyone about her new role as Granny Cyn! Whether that was an appropriate name, no one was quite sure, but they went along with it.

No one mentioned the empty seat that had been reserved on the other side of Pete. Tilly insisted on always reserving a spare seat wherever she played.

However, everyone knew of its significance, a tribute to Jo who could not be there in person but who lived permanently in Tilly's heart.

Tonight was a celebration. It was an accumulation of what some would describe as, blood, sweat, and tears. Tonight was all about the future. Not forgetting the past but putting it in its rightful place, a bright, successful future, full of hope and joy.